Preface - Предисловие

Then a bear came up and asked him, 'Hello, Dog, why are you lying here?'

'I have come to die of hunger. You see how unjust people are. As long as you have any strength, they feed you and give you drink; but when your strength dies away and you become old they drive you from the courtyard.'

'The Bear, the Dog and the Cat' from *Russian Folk-Tales* by Alexander Nikolaevich Afanasyev

'Let us stop obeying the tyrant: let us announce our intentions not just with our bellowing but with simultaneous jumping and head-butting ... all domestic creatures whom the human has enslaved will rise up for freedom from our shared tyrant. We will cease all our internal fighting, all petty disagreements between individuals, and at every moment we will remember that we share a common enemy and oppressor.

'We will achieve equality, liberty and independence; restore the overthrown and trampled dignity of all living animals; and bring back those happy times when animals were still free and not trapped under the cruel reign of humans. Let us go back to those blissful old times: all the fields, meadows, pastures, groves and wheat fields will be ours, and we will have the right to graze, buck and playfully butt our heads where ever we want. We will start living in total freedom and absolute happiness. Long live the beasts! Down with mankind!'

Animal Riot by Nikolay Ivanovich Kostomarov, 1879

1

Prologue - Пролог

Ekaterinburg, July 4, 1898

Dear Sister,

Before I return to St. Petersburg, I have the most amazing tale to relate to you from my time at Uncle Vanya's. You remember my student friend, Vasily Alexandrovich, whom I brought to dinner one night at Papa's? Well, who should have been invited to stay for the summer at our Uncle's neighbour, Court Councillor Kedrov, but Vasily himself? Vasily, as it turns out, is a kind of third-cousin of Kedrov's and enamoured of his daughter. As soon as we realised we were staying no more than three versts from each other, we made it our custom to go out riding most days to the villages around: north, south, east and west, as it says in the folktales.

It was on one of these journeys that we came upon a wandering yurodivy who told me the story I have written down for you here, one so vivid it seems to me more like a prophecy than the bedtime stories, as told to us by our nurse, when we were children.

Have you heard of the holy fools, who on occasion journey deep into the Siberian forest, communing with the tribes there and seeking God in the wilderness? Well, one day, we stopped at an inn to water our horses and ourselves, of course. In the gloomy interior, sitting quite upright by the fire, his eyes piercing bright through the darkness was Grigory. I will not give him a title, whether he was monk or priest I did not enquire, for it seemed an insult to ask. When he spoke to us, his words mesmerised. Even Vasily, that hot-headed fool with his dangerous socialist ideas, fell quiet and was respectful to a holy man

ANIMAL CO-OPERATIVE

OPERATIVE
Скотский Кооператив: Сказка

ROBERT ADAM

ISBN 978-0-46362-584-2 (ebook)

ISBN 978-1-09195-967-5 (paperback)

CONTENTS

of the Church.

But I run ahead of myself. We had started a conversation at the inn with a merchant's clerk on the subject of land reform, and whether Russia should adopt the Western custom of the peasants owning and farming their own land, instead of being tied to the communal obshchina as they mostly are today. Vasily is opposed, he claims that the obshchina is a model for the kind of society he and his friends wish to build in Russia and fears that encouraging the peasants to seek the freedom to run their own individual affairs will undermine his movement.

As the conversation at the tables grew heated, I had strong sense of a presence behind me, drawing our words into himself. We both turned, and that is when I saw Grigory, sitting silently, listening in the darkness. Once we became aware of him, our arguments broke down, their threads were lost, and we began to make even less sense to one another than before.

Eventually, we could bear it no longer and went to sit with the holy man to ask what he thought on the topic. He made the sign of the cross, folded his hands, and merely said that he was on a journey to bring a message from his travels to our Little Father. We naturally asked him if he was permitted to share his words, but he smiled enigmatically and said they were for the Tsar's ears alone.

We asked him if during his wandering he had heard any unusual stories which he was allowed to tell us. He smiled again and in turn asked us, if we had ever heard of the root of the bitter gallwood. According to Grigory, on the fringes of the Empire where the writ of the Holy Church does not run, the tribal shamans, as they call their witch-doctors, drink an infusion of this plant which allows them to have visions. At this point, Grigory took the smallest piece of a black tarry substance out from a greasy leather pouch he kept against his chest. He carved off a still smaller piece with a silver knife inscribed with characters I did not recognise, but, if I had to guess, would be a kind of ancient Georgian script and invited us to chew the morsel. This I did, finding it exceedingly bitter, and disappointingly, without affording any discernible trance-like effect. Grigory merely smiled again and said it was because of my lack of faith in his words, at which I felt a deep guilt. I swear, Sister, that yurodivy could convince even dullest and most unimaginative peasant that black is white. If he is ever allowed into the presence of the Tsar, I would not be surprised to hear that the Emperor of All Russia had been mesmerised by him too.

Anyway, now to the story he told us – here are his opening words, as far as I remember them. The impression of them is still quite clear to me, despite the passing of a week, even if the language is not familiar somehow.

'You ask what will come of it, if the peasants are given their own land? As I sat in the hut of the shaman last winter, we discussed many things, the ever-changing seasons, the nature of the wolves in the forests, whom the tribe believe are the spirits of evil ones doomed to roam the earth. We meditated on the nature of the spirits of the other animals too, and how we humans came to assign their characters, such as the noble horse, the foolish sheep and the angry bear.

We considered too the Empire and its peoples, for which a obshchina and its peasants are but a miniature. We considered what would happen if the Tsar and his subjects, peasants and their obshchina were one day separated apart from each other. We all know that the Tsar has been given to Russia by God to rule over us, but is this not also simply the natural order of things, that the strong rule over those too weak to defend themselves?

And what of the animals? What if, one day, they also overturned the natural order of things and ruled the grasslands, the forests, and the rivers instead of their human masters? Who amongst them would eventually rise up to rule over all?

As I drank deep of the draught of the bitter gallwood,

my spirit wandered far from my body, into another time and another place, where the obshchinas were no more and all the peasants had become kulaks, each with their own lands.

I do not understand everything of what I heard and saw on my journey through the spiritual world, and I do not think it is a message for Holy Russia at this time, it is perhaps meant instead for another time and for another people.'

Sister, I have spent the past week writing down for you what Grigory told us at the inn, but in my own words and style. I enclose the manuscript with this letter and hope it will provide you amusement until my return to Piter at the end the summer.

Your loving Brother,
Yury

Chapter I - Глава I

Once upon a time, in a certain country, a certain Governor joined the Tsar of that land on a quest to recover the Second Rome. Before he left, he called together the kulaks in his county and instructed them thus.

'Orthodox people, hear this. I go to win the holy city of Constantine back from the Turk. While I am gone - and I shall not return until my task is complete - the Tsar has granted that no-one shall be appointed in my place. Instead, I require that each of you administer fairly the lands you have been entrusted with, that you treat your farmhands and even your very animals with compassion. For if you do not, your position shall be overturned and instead the animals will rule over you.'

As you may guess, as is the way with people, some of the farmers listened and took the Governor's words to heart and some did not. Once he had gone overseas, in his absence they began to maltreat their servants and livestock most cruelly. As this is a fairy story, you may also guess what happened next.

One night the animals were given the power of human speech and comprehension of the same. The next morning, as they were being driven out to the fields under the whips of the overseers, each beast, as if acting as one, rose up, bit back, and eventually drove off from their farms the wicked kulaks who had ignored the Governor's warning.

After the humans were gone, all the animals on each of those farms assembled in their barns and discussed what to do next, and how their lives should be organised. Some argued that one animal should simply be chosen to replace the farmer. Others asked who would choose this animal and how often? - for they also asked, what would happen if the new leader turned out to be no better than the human who had gone before?

This is indeed what happened on Krasnaya Farm, where the pigs (the most intelligent animals there) took charge and one of their number ran it in much the same way as the kulak had done, but with greater cruelty and less freedom, if that were possible. They justified their action by pointing to the necessity of preserving at all costs, Animal Rule, as they called it, to give it a title.

On the neighbouring farm of Chernopol, the farmer, Nemetsky, was also notorious for the harsh treatment of his animals. When they rioted against their hated master, he blustered and threatened, but ended up barricaded in the cellar of the farmhouse with a few of his more loyal farmhands. After three days, though, listening to the Chernopol animals marching round and round the farmyard overhead, he turned his gun on himself rather than face the consequences of his crimes.

After Nemetsky was gone, over that summer the farm split into two factions. Nemetsky's pigs knew secretly that, in fact, the pigs on Krasnaya Farm already ruled over the other animals there and believed that they should be in sole control of Chernopol too. They managed to convince half the animals that pigs knew best how to run a farm, pointing to the overflowing bran bins and hay mangers at Krasnaya Farm, the existence of which, they claimed, every enlightened animal knew to be a fact. The other half were suspicious, claiming that if the Krasnaya Farm animals really had it so easy, then all the other farms ruled by the animals would surely have copied them already, instead of still being in debate as to the best form of farm administration. But after some time, across the majority of the farms, the animals did indeed settle on rule by a council, known as the Animal Committee, led in turn by a

Chair. At Chernopol, it was proposed that the Committee be chosen by simply giving each animal a vote, to be cast once each year. This had been the immediate cause of the dispute with the pigs, who had claimed that only they should be allowed to vote, on behalf of the willing lower animals, of course.

The only solution seemed to be to divide Chernopol in two. The pigs took the eastern half, from the wood up to the boundary with Krasnaya Farm. The pigs' half included the farmhouse, so for their headquarters, the animals of western part had to make do with two farm labourers' cottages, which they knocked into one. The new farm office stood on the banks of Chernopol Brook and was somewhat damp in winter, but it would have to do until that day came when Chernopol might be reunited.

The very first Chair of the West Chernopol Animal Committee was an ancient cat named Merlin, who had been chosen by the animals out of respect for his longevity. In the years before the Animal Riot, he had avoided Nemetsky's short temper by hiding deep in the darkest corner of the barn when he heard the approach of jackboots. He was a wily animal, a survivor, even without the help of his nine lives. He knew that, for now, the animals needed the knowledge of Nemetsky's workers on the use of tools designed for human hands, especially given that some of the most productive fields lay in the eastern half of Chernopol. Merlin was even prepared to forgive the farmhands who had stayed on with Nemetsky in the cellar, which caused consternation to those animals with friends who had died in the Riot. He explained it as a necessary, temporary measure until the West Chernopol animals had adapted the farm equipment for themselves, and that the farmhands would soon be expelled - but they never were, at least, not as long as Merlin was Chair.

Not all of the kulaks had been cruel at all times, and on some farms the change to Animal Rule was less severe than on others. On the rambling Belostrovo Farm, the animals had indeed taken charge from their farmer, Korolsky, in an initial burst of enthusiasm, but without any serious violence (apart from that to a black hen, who had been mistakenly trodden on by a horse in the race to close the farm gate and prevent Korolsky from having any ideas of escape). Their enthusiasm for Animal Rule had even extended to taking most of Korolsky's human possessions, including a particularly fine set of silverware, which they then claimed would be mutually owned by all the animals. But their ambition stopped there - far from Korolsky being expelled, he even remained living on in the farmhouse for the time being with a small allowance and the ceremonial title of 'Chief Farmer'. The farm's work orders and regulations were even still signed in Korolsky's name, much to the disgust of the newly-minted Animalists of Chernopol, both East and West. But the animals of Belostrovo did not seem to mind. For the first few growing seasons after the Riot, the Animal Committee even alternated the management of the farm with Korolsky's former overseer. This did not make for continuity, or for a prosperous farm, but Belostrovo muddled through somehow, even at the cost of selling off some of its outlying fields.

Other large farms had carried out full Animalist revolutions, though. Frantsiya Farm bordered the westerly part of Chernopol. There, the farmer during Nemetsky's day, Klemansky, had been in bitter dispute with Nemetsky over the exact course of the boundary fence between the two estates. Oftentimes, Klemansky would send men by night to move the fence closer towards Chernopol Brook, and the following day Nemetsky's men would move it back again, usually with kicks and blows. After Nemetsky's demise, the fence stayed where Klemansky had last moved it. Shortly after that, a Charolais bull named General had led the Animalist liberation of Frantsiya Farm, before retiring in a fit of pique when the other animals insisted the farm should be run by an Animal Committee, instead of himself as a directly elected Chair.

All in all, life was better now for most of the animals in the county, even, to a degree, those of Krasnaya Farm. Despite the claims of the pigs that they were best-suited to running a farm, the animals there always seemed to have less feed and had to work longer hours than those on other farms, no matter what the pigs did to try to increase the rate of production. But this was not apparent outside Krasnaya Farm, given the pigs' secretive nature and hence the farm's limited intercourse with the rest of the county.

True, Chernopol had indeed suffered grievously in the Riot and the subsequent partition. In the confused days leading up to the final separation, the pigs had burnt the barn and the grain store before retreating east. Then, they had immediately built a stout fence, backed by a deep ditch, between the two halves of the farm to ensure that the animals in the east could not change their minds about having allowed the pigs to take charge there and leave.

Compounding West Chernopol's problems was the bull from Frantsiya Farm, General. Before he retired, he had tried to convince the Frantsiya Farm animals that West Chernopol's weakness was their opportunity to take over parts of it for themselves and had even claimed that the natural division between the two should be Chernopol Brook. To that end, he planted himself and the cows on the water-meadow between the actual boundary fence and the stream, claiming that Nemetsky's previous depredations meant the Frantsiya Farm animals were owed the grass there, more luscious and sustaining than anything they could find in their own fields.

Merlin, the West Chernopol cat, pondered long and hard on this. In the evenings he would walk out alone from the new farm office, up and down the banks of the brook, looking over to the cows on the other side munching away contentedly, and wondering how he could ever get the meadow back, let alone recombine his farm with East Chernopol one day.

One early autumn evening, as the first stars were peeping out of the sky, he heard a rustle in the hedge overhanging the stream. To his surprise, out wriggled Abraham, a pig from Frantsiya Farm, who in times past had toured the county as a show pig under his full title, 'Old Father Abraham', and had thus spoken with many different animals from the other farms. Abraham was of the opinion that thanks to his wide experience, he now knew better how to run a farm than any other living animal. But he kept his opinions largely to himself, and so far, had shown no interest in proposing motions at the barn meetings on Frantsiya Farm, or in standing for election to the Animal Committee there.

Abraham now addressed Merlin thoughtfully. 'I see you, brother cat, walking to and fro each evening, burdened by the weight of responsibility. Would not our task be so much easier if the farms were left entirely to the direction of us higher animals, equipped by nature with greater intelligence, and working together with a single purpose? That way we could avoid the crude squabbling, as the humans do, over fields such as the one behind me.'

Merlin looked at Abraham with narrowed eyes. 'Perhaps, brother pig, but that does not change the fact that West Chernopol owns this field, and I fear we shall soon have no choice but to go to the County Tribunal at Vilagrad and put our claim before human judges - to the shame of all animals.'

'What if there was another way? What does Frantsiya Farm want, but merely to ensure that the water-meadow grass is not used to feed Chernopol cows, and that their milk is not then fed to your dogs' pups to make their teeth and bones grow stronger? What if we were to propose to our respective farms that a joint Grass Production Co-operative should be formed, where grass and hay from the water-meadow would be harvested together and shared together?'

Merlin continued to look suspiciously at Abraham,

trying to deduce if this was a secret stratagem of General, whom, in the twilight, he could see sleeping under a tree on the far side of the meadow. 'And who would manage such a venture? We animals are still learning human ways and have enough trouble merely choosing Committee members at our barn meetings as it is, without having to secure the agreement of the Frantsiya Farm animals to grazing arrangements for the meadow too.'

Abraham replied, 'To lead your proposed co-operative you will need to appoint an animal who has never before sought office and so would not be seen as threat to the current Chairs. An animal who is well-travelled, at ease speaking not only with the animals of both farms but also with the humans to whom you will eventually sell any surplus hay and silage which the water-meadow might produce. And above all, it must be a higher animal, such as a cat, a horse, a bull, a pig, or even a crow - but no dogs, of course.'

'And why should that higher animal be you?' asked Merlin.

'Because I have come to you with my idea and not to General. Think of this as a way to ensure that if General is ever chosen by our animals as their leader, it will be me and not he who controls the production of the water-meadow. But the arrangement can only work if the Co-operative's management is clearly independent of the Animal Committee of each farm.'

Merlin did not accept or reject the idea there and then. In any case, Abraham needed to get the Frantsiya Farm animals to agree to it too. However, when encouraged by like-minded friends, he refused to speak at their barn meeting, claiming the other animals would only misinterpret his intentions if he had to explain his ideas to them clearly.

Instead, Abraham laid careful plans to convince the animals of both farms, but by doing so indirectly. Firstly, he persuaded an acquaintance from his show pig days, a bulldog from Belostrovo, to come to speak at the Frantsiya Farm Animal Committee and warn them about the upcoming court case. The bulldog pointed out in a gravelly voice that if the County Tribunal made a judgement on the boundary dispute, then other decisions made by animals could be open to revision too, such as the removal of the human farmers (Korolsky excepted of course). As told to him by Abraham privately, he informed the committee that the case was expected to be heard at any time, and that Merlin had said Frantsiya Farm had two days in which to come up with a suggestion, acceptable to West Chernopol, which would allow them to withdraw their case.

None of the Frantsiya Farm Animal Committee had any idea what that offer might be, but they did know that the grass-eaters among them prized the wide water-meadow above all other fields and were loath to simply give it up without an attempt to hold onto it.

Then, the very morning when the deadline was due to expire, Abraham explained his plan for what he termed a 'Grass Production Co-operative' to another of his friends, an older pig on the Frantsiya Farm Animal Committee named Clefthoof. Clefthoof had been appointed to deliver the offer to West Chernopol, but, as of that morning, still had no idea what he might be able to tell them.

Abraham told Clefthoof not to warn the other animals on the Frantsiya Farm Animal Committee what he was about to say, but instead to go to the tall tree in the middle of the water-meadow, within earshot of West Chernopol's farm office, and announce it from there.

Clefthoof placed his front trotters on a fallen branch and began to declaim in a querulous voice, reading from Abraham's script.

'Brother animals, even in the short time of our freedom, we have begun to copy and fall into the habits of our former human masters. Why is hoof raised up against paw? Why does the bark of the dog cause the hen-chicks to tremble in their roosts at night? Why should we carry on the feud of Klemansky and Nemetsky? Let us rather, in a spirit of Animal Rule, share the grass which grows in the water-meadows of both Frantsiya Farm and West Chernopol. Let us cut the hay together, let us store the fodder in each other's barns, and let the ruminants among us partake in the silage as brothers and sisters for the benefit of all.'

Afterwards, the speech was known as the Clefthoof Declaration. Everyone in a small circle of higher animals knew that such cleverness was the work of Abraham, but he did not receive any credit for it. Puzzlingly, to some of those animals used to the contests for Chair of the Animal Committees, he did not seem to mind this at all.

Merlin heard the fine words. He knew that the water-meadow lay almost entirely on West Chernopol's land and that his farm would be doing most of the sharing. But against such a noble appeal, he also knew he would be unable to convince the West Chernopol animals to question the details of the offer. He knew too, that this was indeed a more reliable way of confirming West Chernopol's ultimate ownership than risking a case at a human court, which might well misunderstand the first such dispute brought by an animal-run farm and be arbitrary in its judgement.

So Merlin announced his intent to drop the case at the County Tribunal and agreed to the establishment of a Grass Production Co-operative at the next West Chernopol Animal Committee meeting, which took place that very same evening. He reminded the animals present that he was the only animal who had resisted Nemetsky's rule before the Riot (albeit from the safety of the barn rafters) and hinted at the respect due to him from his great age. As usual, no one demurred with his decision - it was a technique he had used on several occasions by now to get his own way.

Abraham did, though, manage to get himself appointed

as the head of the Frantsiya Farm delegation to West Chernopol, sent to agree the practical details of the administration of the Co-operative. As he was the only animal from the delegations of either side who had really thought through how this might be done, it was decided that the natural course of action would be to allow him to write a constitution and make him the first Secretary.

The appointment was confirmed, and General, grumbling, agreed to follow Abraham's grazing rota and move off the water-meadow by the end of the month. In any case, he was no longer comfortable grazing there, now that the strip of land was clearly part of West Chernopol again. Indeed, he was vaguely irritated each time he saw the boundary fence, repainted in the West Chernopol colours, with alternating black and red uprights.

Merlin proposed that Abraham should be given one of the farm labourer's outhouses at West Chernopol's headquarters as his office, but this was not entirely to the pig's liking.

'An outhouse overhanging Chernopol Brook will not suffice. A venture of this importance will require an additional office, on Frantsiya Farm, to ensure the equitable treatment of both parties, and to allow it plenty of room to expand.'

'Expand?' asked Merlin.

'Other farms, when they see the success of the Co-operative will surely wish to join, farms with like-minded, higher animal, leaders. And when we are successful, why then stop at grass? Think of the possibilities if we were to pool the production of eggs and milk, and the growing of roots.'

'But that would mean that the Co-operative would gradually run more and more of each farm's affairs.'

'And that is a good thing, brother cat. Why should our peace and prosperity be left in the hands of ordinary animals? Look at Belostrovo, where they cannot decide from year to year whether it is better to grow the same crop everywhere at once, or to allow animals to manage individual fields as they see fit.'

Merlin agreed, but he had not lived this long and survived Nemetsky by being easily fooled by grand-sounding plans and promises. The Frantsiya Farm animals were becoming wary too, after their initial enthusiasm. For Abraham's use they gave over the stable by the barley field, in which used to live the pet pony formerly ridden by one of Klemansky's daughters. They also insisted that Abraham spend every other month working there, when he was not at West Chernopol, so they could keep their eyes on him.

In fact, Abraham merely spent most of the next couple of years trying to convince the animals at some of the smaller farms surrounding Frantsiya Farm and West Chernopol to join the Co-operative, and with some success. He offered to take under his tutelage any of the animals from the constituent farms who were willing to learn from him, whether he privately regarded them as being higher animals or not. At the Barley Field office, he had part of the stable converted into a classroom where he quietly taught his philosophy of beneficent higher animal rule, which he now named 'Pan-animalism'.

Chapter II - Глава II

Abraham was delighted that he had managed to persuade the animals to adopt his idea of a co-operative, without them realising his true plan, and had that he had control of the Co-operative right from the very start, so as to set it on the right path to fulfil his dream.

He explained to the animals he had taken on as apprentices, that he had heard that many, many years ago, before there had been a Governor, there was a Count of Vilagrad, whose lands had stretched from one side of the county to the other in one unbroken estate.

'One day, the higher animals will put those holdings back together and rule the county for the benefit of the lower animals, who often do not know what is best for them, and without our constant watchfulness would revert, perhaps even,' here he paused for dramatic effect, continuing in a sibilant whisper, 'into wildness.'

The younger animals yammered and yowled. Such a fate must not befall the animals, even if it required forbidding the lower animals from speaking up at barn meetings or having any say in how their farms were run - in contradiction to the tenets of pure Animal Rule, which were to treat all animals as equals. This proposal did cause them some passing unease - most animals were proud of the fact that they had shown the humans how every animal, of whichever species, could be trusted to work together for the common benefit of all.

This was why Abraham called his philosophy 'Pan-animalism' - it sounded somewhat like 'Animal Rule' but was not exactly the same. The subtlety was that over time, his Co-operative would reassemble the former Count's land-holdings by weakening the individual farms through the gradual removal of their rights to direct their own affairs – rights which were exercised jointly by all the animals on each farm today. Instead, these powers would be placed into a structure, superior to the farms, and in actuality controlled by a select number of higher animals, appointed by Abraham and his successors. On the surface, the farms would together decide plans for the Co-operative, but by majority voting only, as far as Abraham could help it. As long as no single farm could determine the outcome of decisions by exercising a right of veto, then the Co-operative's Secretariat would be left holding the true levers of power.

For the Grass Production Co-operative to grow in overall influence, in turn reinforcing the natural bias in its governance in favour of the Secretariat, the Co-operative would have to constantly find new areas of farm life to add to its activities. This growth Abraham called the Clefthoof Plan, to make sure everyone knew that he was not behind it.

The choice of the first new area seemed obvious to Abraham. Unlike him, the pigs of Krasnaya Farm were quite shameless in their manipulation of others - as almost all the animals at every other farm had now come to understand, with the exception of East Chernopol. There, the Krasnaya Farm pigs had even begun to directly appoint the Animal Committee of the smaller farm. At the East Chernopol barn meetings, through a combination of lies and fear, the animals would often deliver more votes for Krasnaya Farm's chosen candidates to the Animal Committee, than there were animals present. In a spirit of comradely mutual protection too, the dogs of Krasnaya Farm roamed freely over all of East Chernopol, especially up to the high fence running between the two parts of the old farm. There they would glower with bared teeth at Merlin, whenever they caught sight of him. For the time being though, growling was all they did.

The growing fear, though, across all the farms, was that Krasnaya Farm would not stop there. The pigs needed to be deterred from any ideas they might have of getting their dogs to worry the West Chernopol sheep grazing up by the Fence or sending their pigeons to peck the corn on Frantsiya Farm. As a solution, Abraham considered that the training and combined leadership of the dogs of West Chernopol and Frantsiya Farm in a kind of Farm Militia would be an admirable idea, one he could easily promote to the Chairs of the Animal Committees at both farms. His reasoning was, given that Krasnaya Farm and East Chernopol had combined their martial efforts, Frantsiya Farm, West Chernopol, and even Belostrovo, would surely wish to do likewise, with the Co-operative the ideal organisation to administer a joint endeavour.

Once again, Merlin was somewhat suspicious of Abraham's real intentions. He did not fully understand why a Co-operative set up to harvest hay needed to have its own Farm Militia but did accept there was some logic in the idea of having a single, larger pack of dogs to defend all the farms. Given too, that it was West Chernopol which was facing East Chernopol directly, he had to be ruthlessly practical when it came to questions of defence. This was Abraham's cleverness - his ideas in specific areas were sound, and thus, individually, were hard to argue against at that particular point in time. But all the while, his longer-term plans remained concealed.

General, though, was another matter. While he was still officially in retirement, he did not shy away from making his feelings about Abraham's proposed Militia known to anyone who would listen. 'This is a preposterous suggestion - will a dog from West Chernopol risk being gored for the sake of a Frantsiya Farm goat? Why should a valiant pack of Frantsiya Farm dogs be permanently kennelled within barking distance of the Chernopol Fence, leaving Frantsiya Farm open to the depredations of untrustworthy Belostrovo?'

He took a breath and then a drink from the trough in the Frantsiya Farm courtyard, looking eye-to-eye with the semicircle of animals who had gathered round while he spoke.

'Much better for us to simply agree to go to the aid of West Chernopol, when they call for it, after we have ensured that any destruction of their hay ricks and hen-houses really has been so bad as to justify our assistance, of course.'

The Frantsiya Farm animals nodded in agreement and began to wonder if having General in sole charge of the farm would be so objectionable after all.

In the end, though, it was Abraham himself who brought about his own downfall. He had ignored the farmyard grumblings of General, believing that the Animal Committees of the two farms would surely admire the compelling arguments of his proposal. But they did not admire the unveiling of the Marshal's sash he had designed for himself, as putative commander of the Militia. The seven golden stars, sewn on a grass-green background, were one extra to the six stars on General's historic straw boater with tassels, originally worn by the bull to keep off the flies in the summer. This was the famous hat he had worn on the final day of Klemansky's overlordship of Frantsiya Farm, when General had stormed the barricades, opening the way for the other animals into the farmyard.

Abraham had clearly overreached with himself, and this time, even he could see it. Rather than bring the whole idea of the Co-operative into question, in bitter regret he resigned the Secretaryship, and faded into the background for several months. However, he did not retreat into full retirement, as General had done - he continued to teach Pan-animalism to whichever animal would listen, both at the Barleyfield office on Frantsiya Farm and at the office by the brook on West Chernopol. And the new Secretary of the Co-operative, a West Chernopol cart-horse named

Rock, continually turned for advice to Abraham, as the only animal who understood Pan-animalism completely. Eventually, despite his senior years, relative to Abraham's other apprentices, Rock did grasp almost all of what Abraham intended. Although Rock was, after his own fashion, as vain as Abraham, he used his plodding demeanour to his advantage, so as not to seem a threat, and soon proved himself almost as adept at explaining and promoting the Clefthoof Plan as Abraham himself.

When the humiliation of his resignation had been somewhat forgotten about, both by himself and by the mass of the animals on both farms, Abraham turned his mind once more to the problem of expanding the Co-operative's reach. He realised that he had been on the right lines with the Militia before, and that he should choose another area of practical benefit to promote the advantages of Co-operative management. But he also realised, that anything which looked like the Co-operative taking on the appearance of a farm in its own right should be avoided, for now.

So, because Abraham was still the cleverest animal on both farms, he came up with a plan to propose not one, but two new areas for the Co-operative's work, one of each which he knew Frantsiya Farm and West Chernopol would be favourable towards.

To Frantsiya Farm, he got Rock to suggest that what the two farms really needed was a windmill, just as had been recently built on Krasnaya Farm. 'Every modern farm needs such a plant - on Krasnaya Farm, I am assured, it is used to drive a dynamo providing electric light to every stall, heating for the same in winter, and power for their circular saw, chaff-cutter and mangel-slicer. But individually, our two farms cannot afford to purchase the designs, let alone build such an installation.' Rock was indeed a somewhat pompous animal and enjoyed advising others, once Abraham had given him the words to say.

For West Chernopol, Abraham had a different

proposal. By this time, a couple of years had passed since Chernopol had been riven in two. The West Chernopol animals had been forced to work harder than on any other farm in the county to overcome the destruction wrought and the loss of the more fertile eastern pastures. But now their hard work was paying off, with the productivity of their own fields, whether sown for wheat or grass, having caught up and exceeded that of both Frantsiya Farm and Belostrovo (the latter somewhat easily). Indeed, for next harvest, they now expected to have surplus hay to sell at the market in Vilagrad. But they could not sell the excess from the water-meadow, as this was solely controlled by the Co-operative. So Abraham suggested, through Rock, that in a spirit of Pan-animalism, the Co-operative take over the sale of all the hay, and the silage too, from every field on both farms. He suggested that the sales would be used to fund the windmill, and as this was a joint project, the Co-operative was once again the natural body to direct it.

This was a much more difficult plan for Merlin to agree to. West Chernopol surely needed to earn the rubles needed for its programme of rebuilding, but control of the business arrangements for selling all of their hay would pass to Rock. Even though the cart-horse had been born a Chernopol animal, Merlin was not exactly sure where his loyalties now lay - to the cause of his own farm, or to that of the Co-operative. And West Chernopol also saw no real need for a windmill either - it seemed to them that the Frantsiya Farm animals merely wanted one to copy Krasnaya Farm, so they could then boast about it to all the other farms, especially Belostrovo.

While the Co-operative's plan was being debated, the harvest came around, and West Chernopol made more money at Vilagrad market from the sale of the wheat and the hay from their fields (other than the water-meadow, of course) than they had thought possible. Nemetsky had run a tight operation and that discipline of hard work, unpleasant as it was at the time, had not been forgotten, to the benefit of the farm now.

Now Merlin began to see the benefits of a windmill to grind the even larger pile of corn he expected in the grain store next year, so their produce could fetch an even higher price at market, pood for pood. But if the farm's output were to grow to such an extent, the idea of having Rock in sole charge of realising the value of their production became even less palatable.

At Frantsiya Farm, on the other hand, the initial enthusiasm for the windmill had receded. They realised it would be many years and cost a lot of money before their dreams could be fulfilled. Instead, they began to see the benefit of a common agent at market, who would ensure that West Chernopol did not get a better price for its hay than they could.

It appeared, that despite the cleverness of Abraham, his plans were stuck once more, because of the small-mindedness of the less intelligent animals on the two farms. Then, help came to him from a completely unexpected source. All this time, Belostrovo had remained aloof from the Co-operative. Although not the best managed farm in the county, it was still one of the largest, and still produced a valuable surplus, for which Korolsky (now living in the gamekeeper's cottage) was grateful, as he was awarded a small percentage from the farm's income each year. Belostrovo's objection was to the very idea that Rock ran the Co-operative without any real supervision from the Animal Committees of the farms, and that his word seemed to be final on any decisions which had to be taken. Until and unless that changed, and the Co-operative was clearly run instead by the farms directly, they wished to have nothing to do with it.

Then the news broke that Belostrovo had lost a most serious lawsuit over water rights, brought against them by a neighbouring farm at the Assize Court in Vilagrad, and that the farm would be forced to sell almost a quarter of its land to pay the damages. Korolsky's grandfather had invested heavily, diverting the course of Chernopol Brook, which, in its lower reaches, ran through Belostrovo. This had allowed him to fill a fishing lake, the envy of the county, and a pond and race for a water mill too - where Korolsky would grind the corn of other farmers for a fee. Indeed, given the worn-out state of its pastures, diverting the brook had kept Belostrovo afloat, so to speak, for many years longer than should have been possible. Whether having to sell off its larger fields would be the end of Belostrovo or not, it was an indisputable fact that its weakness had tipped the balance of strength away from the western farms towards Krasnaya Farm and East Chernopol.

Belostrovo's new problems could not be ignored by West Chernopol and Frantsiya Farm for another reason. Korolsky's water mill had been where the other two farms had sent their grain, on occasion, but, following the lawsuit, it was out of commission because Belostrovo could no longer afford its maintenance. Both the other farms now agreed that it was time to start buying the parts and surveying a site for a shared windmill. Abraham's strategy had worked again, the Co-operative was the only joint organisation of the two farms, available to run a common enterprise of such importance. The quid pro quo, of course, was that the farms had to give Rock control of their sales at market to finance the work. As neither farm was completely trusting of the other, it seemed like they had no real choice, but to agree to an expanded Co-operative to carry this out.

With great fanfare, the renamed 'County Farmers' Co-operative' was announced. Abraham had wanted to call it 'United County Farms', but Rock pointed out that this would reveal Abraham's ultimate plan too clearly, and that the prospect would scare off those who still clung onto the labels of 'Chernopol animal' or 'Frantsiya Farm animal', given them by their erstwhile human masters. In order to award the new venture with the dignity it deserved, Rock had the old Co-operative's offices, both on Frantsiya Farm and on West Chernopol, greatly extended and improved, with an additional storey added to each.

Little by little, even though Rock had suppressed the planned name, Merlin began to understand where Abraham's Pan-animalism might end, but the destination seemed so unlikely and so far-off that it did not seriously trouble him.

Chapter III - Глава III

Frantsiya Farm was in crisis. Klemansky had inherited a farm in the next county from a relative on his wife's side, but this was now the cause of a succession of increasingly bitter disputes on Frantsiya Farm. The animals in the next county had also decided that they should run their own affairs, like every other farm which had rebelled against the humans, instead of continuing under a manager sent to them by Frantsiya Farm. They claimed that Frantsiya Farm was acting no differently in this respect than Krasnaya Farm was towards East Chernopol. However, a faction amongst the dogs at Frantsiya Farm violently disagreed, claiming that the fields of the other farm were simply Frantsiya Farm fields which happened to lie in another county. They had gone there on their own initiative, against the will of the Animal Committee (who were minded to withdraw Klemansky's claim of ownership), to stamp out the unrest, but this only made the rebels more determined to break free.

The only animal with the authority to bring the dogs to heel, so to speak, was General. He was happy to be asked to come out of retirement to do so and very happy that the Frantsiya Farm animals had been forced to recognise their mistake in not letting him run the farm right from the days of the Riot. He tricked the dogs into inaction, confusing them by being simultaneously for and against the independence of the other farm, until it was finally too late for them to stop it happening.

Afterwards, basking in the glow of the approval of almost all the other Frantsiya Farm animals, he persuaded them to elect him 'President-Farmer' (an Animalist title, quite unlike Belostrovo's Chief Farmer) for the next three years at a stretch, with the right to suspend the Animal Committee if they started to bore him. Having arranged the administration of Frantsiya Farm to his satisfaction, General turned his attention again to West Chernopol and to the County Farmers' Co-operative.

General had not forgotten, let alone forgiven, Abraham's slight to his pride in seeking to control the dogs of Frantsiya Farm, and worse, that the pig had awarded himself an extra star to those on General's straw boater. Ever since, General had taken to wearing this hat at each formal farm occasion, to remind the animals that he, unlike Merlin or Rock, had actually fought the humans.

In all this time General had not yet seen the Co-operative at work, so decided one day to take a closer look at how Rock conducted the sales of their surplus produce (which now, it had been decided, would include roots along with hay and silage). Late in the afternoon next market day he ventured out to Vilagrad to catch the tail-end of business, just as the market was winding down. Going into the town of the humans was still a thing almost no animal did, mostly, the farms acted through agents who came to them instead. This meant that the few of them who did venture off their farms to understand the affairs of the wider world had an advantage when it came to speaking at Animal Committee or in barn meetings.

Before General had got very far down the lane, he was met by a most strange and disturbing sight. Up from the town came Abraham, driving a cart and wearing a flat cap in a nod to his human customers. But more shocking still, was the sight of Rock between the shafts. The three animals looked at one another, before Abraham hastily spoke. 'Ah my dear General, this is not as it appears, I assure you. Every Saturday, Rock especially asks that he pulls our cart, saying he needs to do so on regular occasions in order to exercise his mighty muscles, the very thing which makes him fully a cart-horse.'

Rock merely nodded in agreement with several tosses of his head. Abraham quickly tied the reins to the hitch and dismounted to walk behind the cart.

'In fact, this is a most auspicious meeting – as you are the first animal to whom I wished to explain the Co-operative's new Equal Rations plan,' said Abraham.

As Abraham talked, despite himself, General became more and more intrigued. Abraham had not persuaded the animals to set up a Co-operative without being plausible and logical in his arguments (according to his own references). Under Abraham's plan, which he attributed to one of his friends, an ox named Genri, the Co-operative would buy on behalf of the farms at Vilagrad market, all of the foodstuffs which they could not grow themselves - such as linseed cake for the cows, sugar lumps for the horses, and biscuits for the dogs. Abraham claimed, reasonably enough, that by buying in bulk, Rock ought to be able to secure a better price than the farms would if they purchased these items individually. The Co-operative would then make an equal allocation per head, across all the farms, to each animal which ate such food.

General remained silent, digesting this new information while the pig rattled on. He began to see two main advantages to the Genri Plan. Firstly, it was well-known that the size of linseed cakes and sugar lumps consumed on West Chernopol were already more generous than those on any other farm. A rebalancing of rations would result in an immediate increase for the Frantsiya Farm animals. Secondly, Frantsiya Farm had many more such animals than West Chernopol who needed this feed and would thus qualify for Equal Rations in the first place. General also knew he had to try hard to keep the Frantsiya Farm animals content, especially the dogs, given the sensitivities over their recent disobedience. The Equal Rations plan seemed to be the answer.

General could already foresee complications, though.

Abraham had lost General when he started to explain the specifications for a uniform density of linseeds in the cakes and the diameter of a standard dog biscuit. But the bull's ears did prick up when Abraham explained how the Co-operative would raise the funds to purchase the rations - by levying a contribution from the sales of every farm at Vilagrad market. Given West Chernopol's growing prosperity, it was clear they would be bearing much of the burden of paying for the new plan. Frantsiya Farm, by contrast, never seemed to have that much to sell at market, not unless one counted the hay from the water-meadow, which in General's mind was still Frantsiya Farm's, never having quite accepted its return to West Chernopol.

On top of the calculations balancing the contributions and distribution between Frantsiya Farm and West Chernopol, there was yet another complicating factor to consider. The Animal Committee at Belostrovo had been looking enviously at the Co-operative for some time, especially since their disastrous lawsuit. The ordinary animals at Belostrovo did not have many strong opinions on whether the Co-operative was a good thing or a bad thing, but their Animal Committee was convinced that what Belostrovo really needed to restore its former level of income was to become part of a bigger combine. The fact that it would be Rock or his agent running their affairs at market and not themselves, either seemed to have passed them by, or else, was secretly the main attraction for them.

General realised, that above all, he had to get West Chernopol to agree to Equal Rations and to Abraham's proposed calculations, before Belostrovo might join. Belostrovo sold almost as much as market as West Chernopol, and it too had many fewer animals consuming bought-in foodstuffs than on Frantsiya Farm. General's animals would thus benefit on both counts if Belostrovo were to join, but not yet - otherwise they might gain the ear of Merlin and argue for changes to the plan, to Frantsiya Farm's disadvantage.

But although General was uncomfortable with Rock (and Abraham) having so much influence in the running of his farm, he was not against the idea of working with West Chernopol as such. In fact, as he walked alongside Abraham, he day-dreamed that if the animals were to appoint himself as Secretary of the Co-operative, in addition to being the President-Farmer of Frantsiya Farm, he would be quite happy to let it carry on its work uninterrupted. But as a longer-term arrangement, he realised it would be better if the Co-operative were to be managed directly by Frantsiya Farm and West Chernopol. To make such a change and to bring the Equal Rations plan to fruition, locking out Belostrovo for the time being, he needed to persuade the Chernopol cat to his point of view.

Saying farewell to Abraham at the gate to Frantsiya Farm, General decided he had no time to lose. Going to his quarters to retrieve his straw boater with the six stars, he went across the water-meadow - which seemed to be producing more grass these days than ever before - then over the brook to West Chernopol.

'My dear Merlin, I am gratified to see the progress of the Co-operative,' for a gruffly-spoken bull, he could be quite charming when required. 'But tell me, surely it should be run jointly by the leaders of West Chernopol and Frantsiya Farm, as its principal constituents, not by an animal appointed from among those trained by Abraham, whose loyalties are unknown? The noble animals of Chernopol, grievously torn apart by civil war, surely have earned the right to freedom and to direct their own affairs, jointly with Frantsiya Farm.'

General said this because he intended that as long as he drew breath, 'jointly' would really mean that he would be in charge. As he spoke, he waxed lyrical about this bright future. 'From Belostrovo's lake to the escarpment on Krasnaya Farm, I foresee a day when all animals will live in harmony as one unit, working together to ensure that the farms of neighbouring counties are reminded of their place and discouraged from undercutting us at market.' He did not explain why the pigs of Krasnaya Farm would agree to this, let alone the pigs of East Chernopol, given how friendly those two farms had become, and also how much they had come to hate both West Chernopol and especially Belostrovo, whom they regarded as outright traitors to their interpretation of Animal Rule.

General concluded his opening salvo with a formal invitation to Merlin to visit Frantsiya Farm, to be given a tour of its richer pastures, and to inspect General's pack of newly loyal younger dogs. They had been disarmed by the old bull's stories of how he himself had fought in the original Frantsiya Farm Animal Riot and by his promise of two and half biscuits per day, just as soon as the other farms had agreed to Equal Rations.

Cats have nine lives for a reason, and Merlin knew not to let himself be taken in by General's blandishments. But as he looked back at the past few years, he could not help a sense of pride at how he had restored the fortunes of the western half of Chernopol, despite the disadvantages they had laboured under at the beginning. General's invitation was a mark of greater respect than he had hitherto shown to any other animal who was not from Frantsiya Farm and was certainly more honour than Rock was wont to give, the cart-horse increasingly given to putting on airs as time passed and the Co-operative's influence grew.

The day of the official visit came, and Merlin's heart warmed with pride as he reviewed the Frantsiya Farm dogs in their matching collars. He complimented them on their display of running along the narrow beams of the barn, jumping down onto sacks stuffed with straw representing the Krasnaya Farm pigs.

By contrast, Merlin's joints were rheumatic now, having lived so long on the damp stream bank, far from the farmyard where he had grown up as a kitten, long before Nemetsky had turned to strong spirits and gone to the bad. But he was charmed by the bull, who was not in the full bloom of youth either. Both of them could remember clearly the time before Animal Rule, and the oppression of the humans. As they reminisced, even to an animal as wise as Merlin, General's words at luncheon sounded seductive.

'How do you propose we take control of the Farmer's Co-operative back from Rock?' asked the cat.

'We are no longer in the era where Abraham gives the orders. Instead of Rock running affairs, the leaders of the constituent farms of the Co-operative should meet every fortnight to decide the price at which we sell our turnips and the rota for fertilizing the water-meadow. Of course, West Chernopol and Frantsiya Farm being the largest members, we will each have a veto and together will have more than half the votes – so we will decide matters on behalf of the other farms,' General did not realise it, but this was exactly the arrangement hated by Abraham, where the big farms controlled the decisions of the Co-operative with their ultimate right of refusal to agree new policies. Abraham called this approach 'Joint-animalism' as opposed to his own, vastly superior, 'Pan-animalism' where his beloved Secretariat could manipulate consensus from behind the scenes, wherever there was majority voting. General continued, 'But we need to go further - instead of the Co-operative organising our mutual defence against East Chernopol, we need to take this step together, to ensure that the Co-operative does not try and again suggest a joint Militia, commanded by Rock.'

At the conclusion of Merlin's successful visit General proposed that to cement their new closer relationship, the two farms should sign a Treaty of Perpetual Friendship. General also insisted that, regardless of any changes to the running of the Co-operative, Merlin and he should agree to meet every three months to agree decisions on things such as the colour of their dogs' collars and the teaching of a common history of the Animal Riots to their younger animals.

Merlin was not entirely sure he had consented to all this but did not want to say 'no' immediately, although he did indeed agree that Belostrovo should be prevented from joining the Co-operative. In the meantime, he promised to at least get the West Chernopol animals to confirm their agreement to the Friendship Treaty at the farm's next barn meeting. When he asked General, on his side, when he intended to get the blessing of the Frantsiya Farm animals, the bull merely smiled and tossed his horns.

In many ways, it did look to outsiders that General was looking forward to a time, as in his speech about animal harmony, when there would only be a single farm. A few of the outsiders, however, recognised that General meant this to be run by himself, and this was perhaps why the West Chernopol barn meeting did not go as Merlin had intended. He was by now a very ancient cat, and a young raven by the name of Jet had plans to replace Merlin once his nine lives were used up, for he showed no signs of wishing to retire, no matter how stiff his limbs were each morning.

Jet argued, that the very reason why the Co-operative had worked until now was because the Chairs of the constituent farms' Animal Committees had let Rock, and Abraham's other apprentices, run the Secretariat without 'interference', as he called it. Jet did not seem to realise that this then meant the Co-operative made its decisions based on the interests of the Co-operative alone. He could see, though, and pointed out to the meeting, that the Friendship Treaty foreshadowed an eventual change in the way the Co-operative would be run, and that the smaller farms would come to resent a Co-operative dominated by Frantsiya Farm and West Chernopol. He also told the animals that such an arrangement would surely dissuade the Belostrovo animals from joining, should they ever be asked. Jet seemed to think their joining a good thing, not realising how important it was to exclude Belostrovo from having a say in the final design of the Equal Rations plan.

Merlin put his proposal for a Frantsiya Farm Treaty of Friendship to a vote of the animals, but Jet's motion to oppose carried the day, thanks to his raven's eloquence. In a burst of enthusiasm, the animals then agreed that although Merlin had merely been the object of General's blandishments, it was finally time for the cat to retire. They voted him an allowance of two dried fish per day and then chose Jet as the new Chair of the Animal Committee.

When General heard the news that his attempt to use a Friendship Treaty with West Chernopol to gradually take over the Co-operative had been halted, he flew into a tremendous rage. He ran up and down the boundary fence between the two farms, bellowing and head-butting its posts from time to time, before eventually calming down. With a face of stone, he marched up to the Barleyfield office on Frantsiya Farm where Rock was working this month, and which now boasted yet another, third storey. In a loud voice, he announced that from now on, Frantsiya Farm would no longer send its surplus produce to the Co-operative for it to sell, and that he would stop attending the supervisory meetings of the Chairs, bringing all the Co-operative's important business of administration to a halt.

Rock now began to panic, the Co-operative was still at an early stage of development, with only a few farms having joined so far, who might now be tempted to go off and form a rival co-operative. He danced from foot to foot, unsure what to do, frantic because Abraham was not there to tell him.

General's bellowing summoned Jet, who flapped over the stream to see what the commotion was about. This was the first crisis which Jet had faced as a Chair - he looked from the angry bull to the cart-horse and back again, quickly coming to a decision.

'What if we agree that the Chairs will not take any decisions at the Co-operative or set any direction to the Secretariat which would be against the declared clear interests of Frantsiya Farm, or any other single farm. But apart from those particular areas, most important to the farms, we allow Rock's successor to carry on making decisions on lesser matters, such as the rota of journeys to market and the other boring administrative tasks needed for the Co-operative to run smoothly?'

Rock pawed the ground with his great forefoot but was secretly relieved to have been offered a way out by the wily corvid. He agreed to Jet's compromise and, with some reluctance, also agreed to resign there and then. This outcome seemed to placate General, and he marched straight out again, forgetting to have the agreement put down in writing.

But that was not General's biggest problem on that day. When he returned to the farmyard on Frantsiya Farm he was confronted by a barricade of hurdles and straw bales erected by the other animals who had heard how Jet had replaced Merlin. They had decided that they too wished to change their elderly President-Farmer, having eventually become tired of General's domineering and his ignoring of the wishes of the Animal Committee year after year.

General turned around once more and that evening slipped through the boundary fence and across the brook for a prior engagement with the Animal Committee of West Chernopol, which he had just remembered about.

When he returned the next day, the excitement had died down somewhat. Overnight, the dogs had approached the animals at the barricades and warned them that the pigs of Krasnaya Farm would seize this very opportunity to take over the management of Frantsiya Farm for themselves. Just how they would do this from the far side of East Chernopol was never quite explained, but it was convincing enough in the febrile atmosphere.

As a compromise, General agreed to hand over the leadership the following year, on the third anniversary of his return. To his credit, he did so, and then was never heard of again. With General's departure, the verbal agreement he had come to with Jet and Rock was also soon forgotten too, much to Abraham's delight.

General's successor was a poodle named Tonton, who, it was rumoured, had also been one of Klemansky's daughter's pets. When anyone suggested this, Tonton claimed indignantly that rather he had always been a sheepdog, which was why he had a woolly coat. The other animals did not quite believe this explanation, but as the Riot and Klemansky's time seemed so long ago, it hardly appeared to matter anymore, as to who had really been on the side of the humans.

Chapter IV - Глава IV

Sunflower was a modern progressive goat. He had little time for the idiosyncrasies of Belostrovo, and their retention of the position and title of Chief Farmer, but he managed to keep this quiet when he stood for election as Chair of the Animal Committee there. For many years, his desire was for Belostrovo to become a constituent of the Co-operative, and he had worked with some success to convince previous Chairs that Belostrovo must eventually take its place alongside the other large farms. He claimed this was the only way to expunge the shame of water rights lawsuit, even though almost all the ordinary animals had already forgotten that event. This was the real obstacle to his ambition - that the Belostrovo animals were generally a contented sort, not given to outbursts of enthusiasm for new concepts, and did not understand the pressing necessity of joining with the other farms to sell their produce at market. They also did not understand that if they really must go into a partnership, why this should be with West Chernopol and especially Frantsiya Farm - their historic rival at many County Fairs for rosettes and prizes. Perhaps this rivalry, they secretly suspected, was really why General had rejected the previous two applications by Sunflower's predecessors to become a constituent of the Co-operative. These rejections only had the effect, though, of making the goat even more determined that his legacy would be as the Chair who finally took Belostrovo into the organisation.

So, on the very day that Sunflower was finally elected, he wasted no time in sending off yet another application form that afternoon.

His first speech to the Animal Committee was naturally devoted to the topic too (despite not having mentioned it once during his election campaign). 'Dear brothers, sisters, and younger animals as well. Joining the Co-operative may seem difficult - but think of the prize. Think of the beneficial Equal Rations the Co-operative will provide to those animals unable to sustain themselves from the bounty which nature has provided to us ruminants.' Here, Sunflower looked at the farm's two dogs and three horses. Those animals, at least, seemed to think that Equal Rations were a good idea, even if they were slightly puzzled as to the change to their current arrangements it would actually entail. 'We should be grateful that the Co-operative has allowed us to ask a third time that we join them. I will have to negotiate hard to persuade them, but it is my highest ambition that Belostrovo will one day be an accepted and influential constituent.' The animals listened politely, but quickly lost interest again - they were not quite sure from the tone of his speech whether Sunflower was referring to himself as being accepted by the wider county society or the farm. However, they took the view that if applying to join the Co-operative kept him busy, then he could not spend his time thinking up new rules for them to obey, as had been his wont when he was a mere member of the Committee.

In the days after his speech, Sunflower asked the ordinary animals what they truly thought about the Co-operative. He was disappointed to find that most of them, if given the choice, would prefer not to be part of it and would rather be left in peace. The speeches of Jet and Tonton, declaiming their respect for each other, which Sunflower had had printed and posted up on the barn wall before his address (although not during his election campaign), had gone over their heads.

Based on the animals' responses, Sunflower came to the conclusion that, if his negotiations to join were successful, he must not make the mistake of asking them if the achievement was worth the concessions he suspected he would have to make on Belostrovo's behalf.

With their scepticism in mind, he made the necessary frequent trips to the Co-operative's Barleyfield office, where in quick succession to the third, a fourth storey had been added to the building, and a single storey side-wing too, for those larger animals unable to climb stairs.

He soon found, though, that each time he went to discuss the application with the Secretary, he was told of something new which Belostrovo would have to agree to, before it could be allowed to join. Of course, this only had the effect of making Sunflower more desperate, which perhaps was Abraham's plan all along.

As he came to learn how the Co-operative worked, Sunflower realised that the edicts which the Secretariat issued in certain areas under their control, such as anything to do with Equal Rations, would overrule any local decision of Belostrovo's Animal Committee. Previously, Sunflower had assumed that if he wished to give extra sugar lumps to the younger animals, perhaps by swapping a linseed cake or a dog biscuit for those sweet treats, he and his Animal Committee could decide this alone for Belostrovo.

To Sunflower's ears, control of those areas by the Co-operative did not seem entirely bad. Indeed, it would mean shorter Animal Committee meetings, as he would no longer have to explain certain topics in tedious detail to the less intelligent Committee members (or even to the ordinary animals at barn meetings). But Belostrovo was proud of its system of farm management, where, just as on Frantsiya Farm and West Chernopol, each animal had a say in choosing their Animal Committee every year. Perhaps the arrangement which Belostrovo had arrived at, with a Chief Farmer, was indeed idiosyncratic, but it had worked for them in the years since the Animal Riot (and even through the crisis of the lawsuit over the water rights, if perhaps less than perfectly at that time).

What worried him much more was a report he was shown at the Barleyfield office, which called for the Co-operative to eventually control the bank accounts of all its constituents, as a precursor to them being merged into one farm. Sunflower quickly buried this report at the bottom of his satchel, getting rid of it one night, deep in the compost heap behind the barn. As a higher animal, he knew it was his duty not to tax the brains of the lower animals with thoughts which would be too complex for them, and only cause distress.

After many meetings, he had finally understood how the Co-operative governed, through edicts which the farms then had to enforce, by having them translated into regulations issued by their own Committees. Sunflower was now even less sure the animals would agree to join the Co-operative, if they were given the choice. And as if he did not have enough to worry about, the Secretary suddenly brought up yet another problem.

The Co-operative had taken over the right to sell at Vilagrad market the surplus hay and silage and, later, roots, eggs and milk from all of the farms. The Secretariat was constantly seeking to expand the definition of what was under its control - for instance, peas and beans had since been classified as root vegetables too, because those plants possessed roots. Now, when they came to review Belostrovo's application to join, they suddenly decided that fish would be classified as eggs, as that was how they had started life (the question of whether fish were animals had vexed the philosophers of Animal Rule for many years, until it was rationalised that fish not being able to speak meant the question could not be definitively determined). Belostrovo's lake was the largest source of fish on any of the three principal farms, so it was unsurprising that the rules were changed, just as Belostrovo sought to join. On West Chernopol, to be sure, a couple of the animals, following Merlin's example, had adapted fishing rods intended for human hands, and from time to time landed the odd trout from Chernopol Brook, but that was as far as it went. Now Sunflower would have to go back and explain that by joining the Co-operative, any animal from West Chernopol, and even Frantsiya Farm if they chose (despite none of the animals there ever having learned the skill), could come to the lake and take whatever number of fish the Co-operative allowed them to. The Secretary explained that there could be a delay (to be negotiated) before the other farms might be issued fishing licenses, but that Belostrovo would eventually have to recognise all permits issued by the Co-operative, no matter how many of these there might be. Sunflower decided that the simplest way to explain this to the Belostrovo Animal Committee (he had long abandoned any ideas of telling the ordinary animals) would be to tell a lie. When he gave his next report, he explained that the Co-operative's allocation of fishing rights to each farm was under discussion and that he had expectations it would soon be settled to satisfaction. The satisfaction of which party he did not say.

Sunflower also knew, that even apart from the fishing question, he would have a hard task to get the final approval of the full Animal Committee to join. He duly arranged for his supporters on the Committee to tour the farm, speaking to the ordinary animals about the supposed benefits of the Co-operative. Although those animals listening to the speeches had no say, of course, in the final decision, Sunflower wanted to give the more reluctant Animal Committee members the impression that there was a groundswell of support for the idea of belonging to a Co-operative. In the end, though, he need not have worried, as the vote in the Committee to approve entry was comfortably won. This was mainly because the Committee had not seen the text of the agreement with the Co-operative, and because Sunflower was supported by certain animals from the other faction on the Committee. These animals were in favour of joining anyway and had kept quiet during the debate so as not to alert their own, opposing, side.

Sunflower's rival for the Chair, a ram named Balthazar, promised that if he was ever in charge of the farm, he would grant all the animals an innovation for Belostrovo which he called a 'Vote of Confidence' on the decision of the Committee to join. But he only offered this to get support for his candidacy from that group within his own faction which was naturally suspicious, not only of Sunflower, but of any animal who sought high office.

After the vote, Sunflower immediately left for a reception which the other Animal Committee Chairs had laid on for him at the Barleyfield office. In the course of time, in addition to an ever-larger headquarters building, the Co-operative had also acquired an anthem, its tune a kind of cross between 'On the Moldavian Steppe' and 'Coachman, Don't Ride the Horses So Hard'. In a state of high excitement, Sunflower hummed this jolly gypsy tune as he skipped along (the anthem did not have any words because no-one had been able to agree on any), his heart bursting with joy.

As he took his place at the polished oak table, which had originally stood in Klemansky's parlour, with the other Chairs of the individual farm Committees, he beamed encouragingly as only a goat can do, showing the other chairs a length of yellow tooth. He then got up to speak, the very first Belostrovo animal to do so at the Co-operative, on what he fondly imagined was an equal footing to the Chairs of Frantsiya Farm and West Chernopol. 'Friends, we must not pause in our drive to turn the Co-operative into everything it should be. I propose that this reception should not merely be a one-off event, but that we continue to meet convivially so that we Chairs can discuss our plans in secret, without the tiresome burden of having secretaries and minute-takers present.'

The other Chairs thought this was indeed a good idea and proceeded to formalise the arrangement by naming these meetings the 'Co-operative Council'. Once something has been named, it takes on a reality of its own, and so it proved with the new Council, which became the de facto inner Animal Committee, or 'cabinet' of the Co-operative, as Abraham likened it to.

Thanks not to being distracted by having their words recorded, the Chairs could discuss freely the report which Sunflower had earlier buried in the compost heap. They agreed that not only should the farms start to bank together (in a joint account, with each farm's savings held in a sub-account under their own control), but what the Co-operative further needed was a common approach to competing with Krasnaya Farm and East Chernopol at Vilagrad market.

Sunflower even suggested that in the far future, they should consider changing the name of the County Farmers' Co-operative to the 'County Farmers' Combine', to have one manager running all the farms in a fair and equitable manner and to turn the joint account into a true single bank account, without sub-accounts, under this future Combine's sole control.

But before the next Council meeting, when Sunflower had intended to expound these ideas further, he faced growing unrest back at Belostrovo, where the lackadaisical management of the farm since the Riot had finally brought about a crisis in its affairs. The immediate trigger for the unrest was a shortage of money to pay for the paraffin in the oil lamps by which the animals read in the evening to improve their minds. A new election was held, and Sunflower's rival Balthazar was narrowly voted in as Chair, promising to restore the supply of paraffin and to hold a Vote of Confidence on Belostrovo remaining a constituent of the Co-operative.

Although Balthazar was not really convinced of need for such a vote, he still did not want to lose it. He, like all the leaders of the factions on the Animal Committee, was generally in favour of keeping Belostrovo's new status as a constituent, even if he was not quite sure what the details of the Co-operative's longer-term plans were.

Abraham was worried that Balthazar was not taking the vote seriously enough. He was shocked that a Chair might even think to give the ordinary animals a say in whether a farm should be in the Co-operative or not but was determined to make the best of a bad job.

He went to Belostrovo on a special visit to Balthazar and together they devised a plan to win the vote. Balthazar would go to the Co-operative's headquarters and argue that the terms of the Equal Rations plan on which Belostrovo had just joined should be renegotiated. Abraham had chosen Equal Rations, as its calculations were so complicated, no-one understood them but him. When the talks had apparently succeeded (and he was going to make sure that they did), Balthazar would be able to return in triumph to Belostrovo and claim a success over the other farms, just before the Vote of Confidence was due to take place. Abraham also met with Sunflower on his fishing punt moored by the side of the lake, taking along two large sacks of sugar lumps. These were provided for Sunflower and Balthazar to distribute as they jointly toured the farm, arguing that the animals could have confidence in the Belostrovo leaders to outfox the other farms, as Balthazar was about to prove.

Accordingly, Balthazar went to the Barleyfield office to demand a reduction in the levy on Belostrovo's produce at market which helped pay for Equal Rations. Discussions immediately got bogged down, however, in arcane details, such as whether a linseed cake was worth three and a half sugar lumps, or if it could be replaced with two dog biscuits in the calculations of each farm's contributions to the Co-operative. Balthazar was puzzled, as he had not fully grasped that Belostrovo would ultimately be paying for Equal Rations, and when it came to it, more per head than any other farm. After many hours of negotiation, Jet persuaded the Council, that, in fact, two and a quarter biscuits were the equivalent of three and fifteen sixteenths of a sugar lump. A breakthrough was declared with great fanfare by Balthazar, and he immediately returned to hold the Vote of Confidence.

In the end, Abraham need not have been so concerned. The Belostrovo animals, by nature somewhat trusting, placid, and averse to change, had been told that as they had already been members of the Co-operative for the past three months anyway, it would be too much effort to leave. They were told that Balthazar had scored a great victory in defending the Equal Rations of their two dogs and three horses. Only a few Cassandra voices claimed that by taking part in an Equal Rations plan and issuing every farm with a license to fish in Belostrovo's lake would result in a new Count of Vilagrad who would arise to take back their farms and their freedoms. The animals simply understood that the Co-operative negotiated the sale of straw and the purchase of dog biscuits on behalf of all the farms, which seemed to be a practical help to Belostrovo, and that was good enough for them.

As soon as the Vote of Confidence had been won, Balthazar went back to the Barleyfield office for the next Co-operative Council meeting. He was somewhat surprised to see that a new resolution had made it onto the agenda, which he had not been aware of - the immediate transfer of all the farms' bank accounts into sub-accounts held jointly with the Co-operative. The Secretary explained to Balthazar that this arrangement, already agreed by Sunflower, would in fact mean that he would be able to negotiate a better deposit rate on their behalf at the Vilagrad & County Amalgamated Bank than the farms could individually. Balthazar was also surprised to learn that the twelve-month delay to the start of the other farms' fishing rights was now only to be six months. Balthazar felt he had no option but to agree to this latter proposal - having just been allowed to join, he wanted to show how supportive the Belostrovo animals could be towards the common endeavour. However, he decided that a joint bank account was a step too far, perhaps because of his rival Sunflower's support for the idea.

Tonton from Frantsiya Farm was most displeased at the thought that Belostrovo would retain a greater degree of independence than the other farms. In revenge he demanded a greater share for his farm from the Equipment Fund, which had also been agreed at Sunflower's last meeting under 'Any Other Business'. This fund was meant to provide those farms, such as Belostrovo, who had fewer animals qualifying for Equal Rations, some recognition of the fact that it was the levies on their sales at market which paid for the benefits enjoyed by the other farms from the plan. Indeed, some ninety percent of what the Co-operative received was spent on paying for Equal Rations for all the farms, but especially Frantsiya Farm. The Equipment Fund, as suggested by its name, paid for modern machinery such as horse-drawn threshers and seed drills, of which Belostrovo, given its dilapidated state, was increasingly in need of as the years went by. Tonton asserted that by not agreeing to participate in the proposed joint account, this was proof of Belostrovo's perfidy and its betrayal of the ideals of the Co-operative. Only increased payments to Frantsiya Farm could mitigate this insult, to which the Secretary and the other farm Chairs agreed.

But as the months went by on Belostrovo, neither the Equipment Fund nor Equal Rations seemed to make much difference to the welfare of animals, even to the few who were meant to benefit directly. If anything, they found that a Co-operative-bought standard linseed cake was slightly smaller in size than the brand they had been used to eating before.

Gradually, a wave of discontent began to grow in the pastures and chicken runs. The mismanagement of the farm had finally become so bad, that the animals who operated the waterwheel driving the dynamo quit in protest, and oil lamps were again rationed to three evenings per week. Finally, the patience of even the Belostrovo animals with their leaders snapped, and they demanded the resignation of the entire Animal Committee. In the subsequent election, they chose a mare by the name of Duchess as the next Chair, the very first female animal to lead any of the farms of the county, east or west.

Chapter V - Глава V

Abraham was delighted that Belostrovo had joined the Co-operative. The three largest farms in the county to the west of East Chernopol were now in his net, and the next phase of his plan was ready to be carried out.

As he approached old age, he was increasingly obsessed with the history of the Counts of Vilagrad and collected whatever books he could find on their lives and the holdings they had built up over time. He was especially fond of telling the story to his young acolytes of how the first Count had famously beheaded two rebellious peasants with a single stroke of his sword. Although the Counts had been human, he dreamed of the day when a higher animal would unify the county into one farm, for the benefit of the less intelligent animals, of course, and restoring the natural order of farmer and farmed (but without any cannibalism).

Abraham decided that the next leap forward on the path to a reconstituted titular county was so ambitious it would need to be taken in two steps. He wanted to firstly institute a system of what he called 'Free Bartering' - where the farms could exchange excess produce with each other at set rates, without going through Vilagrad market and paying taxes to the human authorities to do so.

For a second stage, he then intended that the Co-operative should expand the scope of this system of trade (for example, by allowing any animal to labour on any other farm, in whichever role they were best suited to, returning home at night to their own stables, stalls and hen-houses). But to ensure agreement, these steps would inevitably require the dilution of the powers at Council of the individual farms. Once diluted, he would then encourage the Co-operative to bring further areas of farm administration under its control, which would require yet more dilution of the farms' powers - and so on and so forth. At this second stage too, would also be established the formal agreement, and the start of the preparations, for the Single Account, which would be put into effect at a still later point in time.

Before he broached the idea of Free Bartering with the current Secretary, he commissioned a report for the Chairs which, surprisingly, talked about the heartfelt need of the animals to barter their produce and to labour on each other's farms in a brotherly spirit of Animal Rule. Abraham was not happy that the animal he had persuaded to author the report did not go as far as he would have liked and propose compulsory service for the younger animals in a Co-operative Militia. But he had learned to be patient and knew he would eventually bring the Chairs round to his point of view, all apart from one.

Duchess had proved to be a very different character, over time, to Sunflower - who still sat on the Belostrovo Animal Committee, just so he could tell Duchess what she was doing wrong as Chair. Although, like the other Committee members, she had originally been in favour of the concept of a Co-operative, once she became Chair of Belostrovo and started to attend the Council meetings of the organisation, she began to understand better how Abraham intended it to work. But she too still did not quite perceive his longer-term plan for an animal to one day wear a Count's coronet. The growing stream of edicts from the Co-operative on matters such as the spacing of mangel-wurzel seedlings and depth of the share when ploughing (for reasons of some new things called 'quality control' and 'standardisation') also disguised this intent through their very banality. The Belostrovo Animal Committee, presented with these boring edicts decided they could save the effort of debate (much as they had enjoyed it when they used to decide these things for themselves) by simply copying out the edicts onto Belostrovo-headed notepaper and stamping them with Korolsky's signature to make it their own regulation. The original edicts were then filed away in a locked cabinet at the back of the office, so that no-one would realise what they had done.

Before Abraham could move ahead with the first stage of his plan, the calculations over Belostrovo's contribution to the Co-operative's funds had to be finally settled. These had still not yet come to a satisfactory conclusion, notwithstanding Jet's mathematical legerdemain during the renegotiation laid on by Abraham for Balthazar. Duchess demanded that as Belostrovo, given its size, had relatively few animals consuming Equal Rations, it should get a special repayment from the levy which the Co-operative took from the sale of the farm's produce at market. After much haggling, over several Council meetings, a figure was settled on. Bizarrely, the repayment was partly funded by the Co-operative borrowing from all the farms, including Belostrovo. To raise the cash to lend to the Co-operative, the farms themselves borrowed in turn from the Vilagrad & County Amalgamated Bank. This meant that Belostrovo did not always claim the full repayment owed to it, because it would have to borrow at a high interest rate from the Bank in order to lend out at a low interest rate to the Co-operative. Regardless of what actual sums flowed around the system back to Belostrovo, one thing had been proven - that Duchess would not easily be persuaded of Abraham's new ideas and might have to be isolated in case she infected the other Chairs with her recalcitrance.

But Abraham had not managed to persuade the animals to create a joint enterprise for the sales of their produce at market (all produce these days, not just hay, silage, eggs, milk and roots) and the purchase of all the foodstuffs they could not grow themselves, though any lack of intelligence.

Indeed, he was easily the cleverest animal, east or west of the Fence, but he had long realised he had to conceal this and instead inspire others to do his bidding for him, as he had done with Clefthoof, Rock, and now the new Secretary, a donkey jack named President. And Abraham's dreams too, of Pan-animalists ruling an animal county were by now proving positively intoxicating to the higher animals. As Abraham himself began his twilight years, a new generation was debating Pan-animalism, utterly convinced that left to themselves, without the higher animals' beneficent guidance, the lower animals would certainly become wild again. Indeed, he now began to have difficulties in curbing their enthusiasm. One of the innovations, which he had persuaded earlier Secretaries to adopt, was a Co-operative Animal Committee, in addition to the Co-operative Council (where the Chairs of the constituent farms' Animal Committees met). The Council notionally sat to agree on policies which the Secretariat, led by President, would then turn into edicts, passing these down to the Co-operative Animal Committee for confirmation. This new committee was elected by all the animals across all the farms, and the representatives became employees of the Co-operative, with double Equal Rations for those who could eat such things, and extra leisure time for those who could not. Spare time was a thing which all the representatives had plenty of, as their only task was to ratify the edicts handed to them by the Secretariat. For sure, there was a formal debate and vote, but as the Co-operative's Animal Committee could not alter the text of the edicts, let alone propose their own edicts in the first place, voting against them made no sense, not if they wanted their pleasant life at the Barleyfield office to continue. The edicts were the precious treasure of the Secretariat, once issued, they were never rescinded, and as Sunflower had realised, overrode any regulations issued by the farms themselves locally. Indeed, as the Secretariat issued more and more of these edicts to the farms, the standardisation they imposed became clearer to see, whether or not it made practical sense for every radish plant on every farm to receive the same amount of water in June.

Nevertheless, some of these Committee representatives were proud, even of the limited work they did do, and wished to do more. They began to agitate for greater powers for the Co-operative (which would lead naturally, as they imagined, to a greater role for its Animal Committee). An elderly pig named Albert, with a group of friends who called themselves the 'Wolf Club', in an ironic tribute to the wildness which they sought to prevent regression to, began to meet and publish proposals to anyone of their circle who would listen. Some of these ideas, such as compulsory participation in the joint bank account followed by a rapid merger into a single account, the abolition of local farm Animal Committees and the management of all the farms to be transferred to the Co-operative, were obviously steps too far. In consultation with Abraham they devised a plan to split their desired programme for the Co-operative's development into two or more smaller steps, as many as would be required to advance with the minimum of dissent.

The Wolf Club did, however, argue that it was time to inspire the ordinary animals with the dream of an animal county, or as they more prosaically argued, the original name which Abraham had wished to use all those years ago, the United County Farms. They drew up designs for a flag, an arrangement of golden hooves, claws and webbed feet on a field of green, the choice of colours inspired by the Marshal's sash which Abraham had had run up, back when he entertained dreams of his own Militia. They also proposed that the animals on each farm should henceforth be encouraged to call themselves 'Co-operative Animals', rather than identifying with West Chernopol, Frantsiya Farm or Belostrovo.

Despite all this activity, the fact remained that they

were still only the representatives of a powerless committee. They needed a sponsor from among the Chairs, and found one in Tonton, who was looking for ideas which would allow him to make his mark on history - perhaps so that people would forget about General's record in the Riot and would not ask what a poodle had been doing on a working farm run by humans. The next step was to get Tonton to appoint another animal to author a report, on behalf of the Council, containing the Wolf Club's ideas. This was duly done, and as the ideas began to take shape, Jet decided he wished to share in the credit too. On the anniversary of the Animal Riot on Chernopol, the animals assembled in the barn, as usual, to hear that year's Chair speak.

'Fellow animals, the time is nearly upon us when we will all salute one flag and sing one anthem - as we in the Co-operative's Council are about to agree the words which will go to the tune of 'On the Vilagrad Steppe'' He flapped across the podium, to see if they would be any more attentive, if he spoke from the left-hand side.

'I have here in my claw a report which clearly states,' here he gave a raucous cough to clear his throat, 'that it is the complex and deeply-felt need of the animals of the Co-operative, that they should become, for the first time, "citizens" of this great venture.' For a moment, it looked to the animals that Jet did not understand what a 'complex and deeply-felt need' was either, but he quickly recovered. 'Above all, we must never forget those animals trapped on the other side of the Fence, under the absolute control of the pigs, left without a say in how the eastern half of what was once our farm is run. It is our duty to strengthen the unity of the Co-operative and perhaps one day provide a new home where both the eastern pigs and the other animals over there will feel completely at their ease.'

Jet stopped speaking at that point and did not go on to explain the detailed contents of Tonton's report, he felt clear in his conscience that he had told the animals enough of what would happen next.

What actually happened was a delicate operation to persuade Duchess to agree to the first stage of Tonton's Free Bartering plan, which now not only was intended to encompass the trading of produce at set rates, but also for the animals to be required to labour on any constituent farm in the role it was deemed they were best suited to.

Duchess was very much in favour of the idea that the farms could save money by dealing directly with each other. She had sought to make economies in Belostrovo's outgoings wherever possible, cutting the milk ration to the younger animals and even going to the extent of selling Korolsky's family silver, which the animals had mutualised at the time of the Riot. She believed that free bartering would eliminate wasteful hoarding of long-lasting foodstuffs, like turnips, as each farm would have the confidence that in times of need they could be easily sourced elsewhere. She was also intrigued, and not at all as resistant as Abraham had feared, of the idea that the animals should be encouraged to work to their maximum capacity by moving to find employment on other farms - as she was naturally suspicious of laziness.

When the Chairs attending the Council needed advice in certain specialist areas, they brought along associates. Duchess was lumbered by her Animal Committee with a sheep named 'Hollow', with whom she had a somewhat fractious relationship. He had the advantage over other animals on the Belostrovo Committee that, as a sheep, he was clearly no threat to the mare – for who had ever heard of a sheep savaging another animal? Hollow's advice was that that Free Bartering would only be agreed to if Belostrovo and the other farms were to drop their veto rights in this area at the Council meetings. He told Duchess that as all the other farms agreed with her admirable vision, she should have confidence that they would all vote with Belostrovo anyway, at any really important meetings. Duchess was suspicious, but did enjoy

Hollow's flattery, however superficially it was intended.

Now very much taken with the idea, she tasked Hollow with writing a detailed plan for produce bartering and labour exchange, which she showed to Jet on the very next occasion he visited Belostrovo. Two weeks later, though, at the next Council meeting she was most surprised when Jet and Tonton presented the text of a 'Common Bartering' plan, in which she recognised most of words as having been written by Hollow for his Free Bartering report. She gave a deathly stare to Hollow, wondering if Jet had simply been crass, or if Hollow had been secretly working for the other two farms all along. Little to her surprise, though, as an addendum to the Common Bartering plan, Jet and Tonton had added the building of a Co-operative windmill (at last) and for standardisation to be directed by the Co-operative in several new areas, such as the pension allowances for superannuated animals.

Duchess thought these additional ideas only meant extra expense which Belostrovo would again be paying for, without seeing much benefit, and was determined to stop them. Fierce arguments at Council ensued until, much to Albert's disgust, President, as planned, removed references to a windmill, telling his allies it would be better to take agreement to Common Bartering now, and seek consensus on the other ideas later. The next task was to formalise the agreement, Duchess wanted the Council merely to issue a new edict, but President knew that, in preparation for the next stage of his plan, he really needed a formal resolution from an Extraordinary General Meeting to amend the Co-operative's constitution with an annex.

Duchess's suspicions of Hollow began to grow, especially over his claim that giving up veto rights in the areas covered by Common Bartering was only a minor issue of administrative simplification. But she desired even more the prize of her ideas being put into practice, certain they were the best policies for every farm on the Co-operative. She duly arrived at the next Council meeting, convinced of her correctness. But without warning, a new item had suddenly appeared on the agenda, a vote, by simple majority consent, to indeed call an Extraordinary General Meeting to work on a new annex to the constitution. Duchess had been ambushed, and although she registered her protest to smirks and snickers from the other Chairs, without her veto, it was to no avail. She consoled herself with the idea that her representatives at this special meeting would be able to steer the drafting of the annex, to limit its scope, and avoid the nonsense of providing every retired cat two dried fish per day (as Chernopol had voted Merlin on his retirement).

When the draft came back, though, she saw President's name at the top of the report, instead of a Chair's representative. Worse, President had got carried away again, and the draft included a statement on the ambition to build not one but two windmills (it was realised that Frantsiya Farm and West Chernopol each needed one for parity of esteem). It also included a new requirement, for all farms to enforce standard feed allowances for every animal, not only for those receiving Equal Rations. Even worse too, the veto rights on those particular areas had also been removed, in addition to the vetoes over the Common Bartering arrangements. After yet more heated argument, the new items were taken out of the text of the Annex - but Duchess guessed it would not be long before they came back in a later document.

To further mollify the mare, President even agreed to put the Citizenship idea in abeyance, much to Albert's annoyance. But he did force through agreement that the annex would commit the farms to promote the 'identity' of the Co-operative, for which he announced a competition to devise a flag and words to the anthem. The flag, it was proposed, would be painted on each farm gate to let visitors know they had arrived at the Co-operative. In fact, given the further announcement that the date of Clefthoof's original speech in the water-meadow, marking the founding of the Co-operative, would become a special holiday on every farm, the animals could have been excused for thinking that the citizenship proposal had been left in, but merely disguised. To round off these provisions, there were also going to be compulsory lectures for the younger animals on how the founding of the Co-operative, shortly after the Animal Riots, had certainly prevented the newly freed animals from losing the power of speech and reverting to wildness.

At last, the First Annex to the constitution was signed by the Chairs. As an afterthought, at the same meeting they signed a co-operation agreement on liaison with other farms in the county, which were not already in the Co-operative. The First Annex was an important first step, but whole episode had merely confirmed President in his belief that he would have to be patient and wait on a Second, Third or even Fourth Annex to achieve Abraham's dream in the fullness of time. As for Albert, in his own idiosyncratic way, he complained that 'a mountain had given birth to a mouse', such was his disappointment at the Annex. But he was at least happy that the first steps forward had been taken since the signing of the original constitution, and later that week died peacefully in his sleep.

Duchess, in distaste, had the new constitutional annex quickly ratified by the Belostrovo Animal Committee, hoping this would be the last time she would have to give into the Council.

Chapter VI - Глава VI

After the triumph of passing of the First Annex to the constitution and the launch of Common Bartering, it was discovered that the Co-operative was almost broke. It transpired that every year, more and more animals had qualified for Equal Rations (especially from Frantsiya Farm), until the Co-operative's overdraft had grown to such an extent that it received an unpleasant letter from the manager of the Vilagrad & County Amalgamated Bank. Given that Duchess had been ruthless in cutting unnecessary spending (as she saw it) at Belostrovo, she had no patience for waste at the Co-operative. In her mind, only two things could be done - cut the quantity of Equal Rations or cut the number of animals qualifying for them. President had a different plan, though – to immediately charge a higher levy on the sales of the farms' produce at market, and for the long term, turn the farms' sub-accounts in the joint bank account into a single account. This Single Account would be under the control of the Co-operative, so he could then spend as much money as he liked.

President was aided in carrying out this plan by Hollow's growing attraction to the idea of Belostrovo also joining the Joint Account (Chernopol and Frantsiya Farm had already done so). He believed that if the position of each farm's sub-account was known to the others, this would ensure discipline and the encouragement of thrift - ideas he knew he could persuade Duchess the benefit of. But of late, Hollow, too, had been increasingly seduced by Abraham's vision. He had begun to think of Belostrovo as being in permanent decline (despite Duchess's cuts resulting in a marked improvement in Belostrovo's own bank balance) and only able to survive as part of a true unified farm. It was at this point, that Hollow began to believe that Duchess and her resistance to Abraham's plans were becoming a threat to Belostrovo's future, and that even if he himself had no ambition to be Chair, she should retire and do so sooner rather than later. While Duchess was still popular with the ordinary lower animals, who kept electing her every year as Chair, the higher animals around her now also began to see that her ideas were, in fact, very backward. They suspected that she did not have their intelligence because she failed to understand what a wonderful effect a joint account would have on Belostrovo's finances.

Unfortunately for Duchess's personal relationship with President, a most embarrassing incident occurred during a Council meeting, held at Belostrovo that month, according to the rota. As Duchess held forth at length, President's head nodded lower and lower, until he was asleep. Just at that point in her speech, Duchess stopped to ask a question of him. Roused from slumber, President had not heard the question and declined to say anything, much to the chagrin of Duchess, who made a snide comment in front of the other Chairs. President soon had his revenge though, when Duchess was invited to address the Co-operative Animal Committee at the Barleyfield office. Much to her disgust, she was heckled by some of the representatives from Frantsiya Farm, who, by contrast, cheered President loudly when he got up on all four legs to speak and cheered even more loudly when he berated Belostrovo for the economies they had proposed in the Co-operative's budget. This was especially galling to Duchess, and she told President frostily, that while in the past she had argued the case for the Co-operative at the Belostrovo Animal Committee, she would do so no longer.

Duchess's parsimony and demands that Belostrovo

should live within its means were now starting to pay off. Strangely, despite this, the farm's accountant, a goat of a mountain breed named Scraggy, had fallen in love with the notion of a Joint Account and now joined with Hollow in insisting that Belostrovo participated in it right away. This Duchess did not fully understand, unless it was that the accountant too had been infected with Abraham's ideas, which she was slowly beginning to get a better grasp of. But to placate her fellow Belostrovo Animal Committee members, she agreed to at least discuss joining the Joint Account at the next Council meeting, but only if the Co-operative's finances were put back onto a sound footing - after all, who would want to be jointly-liable with a Co-operative in danger of going bankrupt?

Although the Chairs all knew that it was really runaway spending on the Equal Rations plan which was the main cause of the Co-operative's mounting losses, President threatened to resign unless the farms agreed to his plan of a higher levy on sales. He asked his subordinates to also threaten to resign from the Secretariat too, but they backed out, much to his fury. Now, suspiciously, at the next Council meeting, Duchess came to his rescue. She agreed, that if Equal Rations were cut back, she would reward the Co-operative's prudence by paying an extra, new levy. But she refused to countenance any increase in the Equipment Fund (which President had also proposed) and was especially angry at the idea that individual groups of animals should be able to apply directly to the Co-operative for these funds and not have to go through their local farm Animal Committee. While Duchess was busy preparing her arguments to persuade President of the error of his ways, in the meantime President had arranged a separate side meeting with Hollow and the other lesser functionaries from the farms attending the Council, to restart the planning for a Co-operative Militia. He had discovered, when he dusted off the original plan written by Abraham when he was Secretary (the one which had led to his resignation), that the authority to prepare for the creation of a Militia had never actually expired. Hollow agreed that the planning exercise was not being started anew but merely continuing, which meant he did not have to tell Duchess.

The other factor influencing President's thinking, as he waited to start discussions on the Second Annex, was the continued and ever-faster growing prosperity of West Chernopol. It seemed that whatever the animals there turned their hands to, they made a success of it. Year by year, this was causing ever more worry to Tonton too, and he began to independently rack his brains for a way to limit West Chernopol's power. It seemed there was only one solution, instead of merely running a joint bank account with sub-accounts, the Co-operative had to accelerate its plans for the Single Account and bring all the wealth of West Chernopol under the Co-operative's control. That way, Tonton believed, he could have President write as many cheques for windmills and special nutritional poodle biscuits as he liked. To Tonton, this seemed only fair - such mutual support was merely to recall the primitive principles of Animal Rule, that all animals should work together in the face of their common enemy, man.

While President's and Tonton's interests coincided, the remaining obstacle to the next step, to force every farm to finally adopt the Joint Account, was Duchess. And while a Joint Account was one thing, even Jet was not overly keen on a Single Account – unsurprisingly, given West Chernopol's wealth. Perhaps such an arrangement might come to pass a very long way into the future, but it would take a great shock to move the Co-operative forward together in that way.

In some ways, though, of all of them, it was Hollow who understood best what the nature of a co-operative, run in an opaque way by a Secretariat, was leading to. He realised that the Co-operative simply had to keep acquiring more powers and distracting the Chairs with its plans, otherwise the ordinary animals might stop to think and question the point of all this activity by the higher animals. None of this perceptiveness helped him much, as Duchess's suspicions of Hollow were growing and growing with every passing week. She had begun to imagine he was plotting for her position, along with Scraggy the accountant, with both of them supported by President in the background. And as further weeks went by, she came to suspect every member of the Belostrovo Animal Committee of murmurings in dark corners of the barn and plots against her.

In response to the demand from President that a single bank account now be discussed before the drafting of the Second Annex, Duchess in turn demanded that only the farm accountants debate it in a special committee - expecting that their natural cautiousness would cause them to vote down the idea. She knew she could especially rely on the accountant of West Chernopol in this, as he controlled the biggest amount of cash on any of the farms. However, she had not counted on President, who, despite never having balanced a budget himself, was somehow installed as the chair of the new Single Account committee, somewhat overawing the accountants sitting under him. President's proposition to the West Chernopol accountant was simple, if West Chernopol were to join the Single Account, then the accountant would control it, with a sign-off authority for expenditure three times greater than Jet allowed him on West Chernopol today. In fact, President made it clear to the accountant, that he need never report to a Chair again, only to President directly. He was even happy for the accountant to add a clause to the Committee's report, whereby no farm would have the automatic right to receive financial assistance, and that once the Single Account was set up, they would only be able to request aid from the accountant himself in triplicate.

Outside the committee room, however, President, like his mentor, Abraham, was discretion itself. The final report and recommendations were to be in the name of another animal, just as the Clefthoof Plan had been, all those years ago. And the report was to be limited to the technicalities of implementing the Single Account, such as the design of the account books and the fee which the Co-operative would charge the farms for the initial transfer - but it would not discuss the reasons for setting up the account.

While the Single Account committee carried on its work, the Secretariat was issuing ever more edicts. President noted with satisfaction that it had sent out more instructions to the farms in the previous six months alone, than in the rest of the time the County Farmers' Co-operative had been established. He knew that if he could only get a Second Annex agreed, incorporating new areas of responsibility, such as the Single Account preparations, then he could argue the same Annex should reduce the farms' existing veto rights, ratcheting up the Co-operative's control even further.

Knowing what the committee was going to report and wanting to leave nothing to chance, President started to help Hollow undermine Duchess's position on the Belostrovo Animal Committee. As chance would have it, as an initiative of the Belostrovo Animal Committee to improve relations with Frantsiya Farm animals, President himself had been invited to address an assembly that week of the Caprine and Ovine Brethren, a mutual self-help society of wool producing animals. He made the claim to the assembled sheep and goats that the Co-operative had only been set up for the sole benefit of lower animals (he rationalised this in his head, because higher animal rule was, of course, beneficial to the Brothers). This was of much delight, especially to the sheep, who from that point on wasted no opportunity to heckle Duchess at barn meetings in favour of the Co-operative.

Duchess, Hollow and Scraggy were now split. They could all predict what President's Single Account committee was going to report but disagreed on what Belostrovo's response should be. The accountant thought that joining the Joint Account would actually be the best way to resist calls to join the Single Account. Hollow wanted to join the Single Account immediately, and Duchess wanted neither. But as Hollow's and Scraggy's interests did coincide, to a degree, they went together to see Duchess, threatening to resign if she did not agree that Belostrovo should at the very least join the Joint Account. Duchess thought long and hard, but made no promises to them, saying they would have to wait to hear her decision.

The day could be put off no longer, President called a meeting of the Chairs to announce the contents of his report. Uncharacteristically, Duchess let the other Chairs speak first, and only got up to respond at the end. When she spoke, to Hollow's delight, she confirmed that Belostrovo would, indeed, enter into the Joint Account arrangement, but carefully did not say when this might take place. Her judgement had been that by not agreeing to a hard entry date, she could show her willingness to support the other farms, but without tying Belostrovo down. But in a minority of one, she was worried how her reservations might play out at the next barn meeting on Belostrovo, now that the Brethren were becoming ever more restless. The lower animals did not see, given Belostrovo's improved fortunes, why she still insisted on making continual savings in the farm's spending and on selling off the remnants of Korolsky's silver service such as the sugar bowl and teaspoons.

On their return to Belostrovo, Hollow was promoted to Deputy Chair, a position which had existed for many years, but had rarely been filled, because it carried no actual responsibilities. To Duchess, it seemed the perfect shelf on which to place Hollow, where he would be under her suspicious eye, but without the ability to cause mischief.

After all the arguments between the three Belostrovo leaders, the months passed, and it seemed, that despite the support of the other farms, the Single Account was to be one of those ideas which the Co-operative Chairs agreed on in principle but would never quite act on. Then, quite suddenly and shockingly, the county was turned upside down with the news that both Krasnaya Farm and East Chernopol had gone bankrupt at the same time, with a sale of assets to pay their creditors set for the following Thursday week.

One day the Krasnaya Farm and the East Chernopol dogs had been doing their patrols of the Fence, on the next it had been trampled down by the East Chernopol animals and the ditch filled in with the broken pieces. The newly-freed animals wandered around West Chernopol in a state of bewilderment at the modern heated stalls with electric light and at the farm's machinery such as the hay elevator and the steam engine.

Jet wasted no time in lodging a bid with the administrators to buy the whole of East Chernopol in its entirety. This he did without any consultation with the Co-operative, much to President, but especially, Tonton's rage. To the mind of Jet, it was a question of natural justice, even if the idea of having to buy back buildings and land which had once been part of their farm was painful. The West Chernopol animals had come to see themselves as the natural successor of the old Chernopol and did not see why it should be the Co-operative in charge of joining the two parts back together. But Tonton was not to be placated, despite the enormous expense West Chernopol would incur on its own to modernise the farmhouse for the Animal Committee's use and to shore up the dam holding back the slurry pond, he was fearful of the greater influence within the Co-operative which a united Chernopol would have. He sent a message to Jet, that unless he agreed to the Single Account, Frantsiya Farm would immediately ally with Duchess and ensure that the next Equipment Fund budget would mean West Chernopol paying for new cowsheds on every other farm before a single ruble went east.

Jet weighed up Tonton's threat, made his decision and agreed that he might, indeed be persuaded of the wisdom of the Single Account. On the outside he was smiles (insofar as a raven can smile), inside, he was determined to have his revenge, for he knew just what President had promised the West Chernopol accountant would be able to do with his new powers.

President now struck while the iron was hot. In addition to releasing the draft text for the Second Annex (which had already been in preparation for some months), he proposed not one, but two new sub-committees. These would report on the immediate adoption of the recommendations of the Single Account Committee and also on the concept of turning the Co-operative into what he called a 'Combine'. Everyone, except Duchess, agreed that a Combine was the way ahead - what the word meant, though, was not clear. One of the Chairs, an ally of President, delphically pronounced that to define such a thing would be 'dangerous'. Despite this vagueness from the Co-operative's Council, almost all the Animal Committee on Belostrovo now began to agitate for combination. Hollow moved among the members, whispering words to undermine Duchess, and encouraging them to tell the lower animals that Belostrovo was being held back by the proud mare.

When they were told this, the ordinary animals on Belostrovo became even more restless than before. They had grown tired, not only of her parsimony, but more generally at her belief, that, on any given topic of discussion, only her views were correct. Just before the next Belostrovo barn meeting some of them ran amok in the farmyard in protest, knocking over pails of milk and demanding the election of a new Animal Committee. Ever more isolated, Duchess decided she would make a limited concession to placate her rivals, and agreed it was finally time to join the Joint Account. In his hubris, Scraggy the accountant agreed that Belostrovo would accept a lower rate of interest on its deposits than any other farm did, so confident was he of the transformative effect the Joint Account would have on its finances.

The concession had given her a brief respite at the Co-operative Council too. In fact, President was actually angry that Duchess had agreed to the Joint Account, as this showed she was not as obstructionist as he liked to portray, so he came up with a new plan to encourage the Belostrovo Animal Committee to topple her.

The next Council meeting was meant to discuss the bankruptcy sale of Krasnaya Farm, and the assistance that might be given to its starving animals. Instead, President put on the agenda a resolution for Combination, forcing the Chairs to take a position there and then, ahead of the start of the sub-committee that was actually meant to meet to agree a position. This did not unduly worry the other Chairs, for the surprise gave them the excuse that they did not have a choice but to agree to President's demands. But Duchess voted 'no' to the resolution, the only Chair from any farm to do so. President was delighted, her isolation on Co-operative matters had been restored, and he knew what the outcome on Belostrovo would be, once the animals there heard the news.

Indeed, this was the trigger for Hollow to resign as Deputy Chair in protest at Duchess's lack of forward thinking in not wanting to combine Belostrovo with the other farms, as the other, more progressive, Chairs wished for their farms. In his resignation speech to the Animal Committee he damned her achievements with faint praise, and the other animals sensed her weakness. Several manoeuvred for position in the hope of succeeding her, but as is often the way with these things, the animal who did take over, Normandsky the all-grey donkey, was the most unlikely imaginable.

Chapter VII - Глава VII

President had engineered the removal of Duchess, and now it was time to complete the draft of the Second Annex, which would set in motion the move to the Single Account, along with the reduced veto powers of the Chairs at Council, turning the Co-operative into a combine.

To help convince the ordinary animals of the constituent farms that the Single Account was a good idea, President proposed to link the Second Annex with a new edict, standardising working conditions across the farms. Field-leaders would now have to consult with the worker animals under their direction as to any changes to rotas, or the length time they spent in each field. What he did not say, though, was that future rules in this area could be proposed to the Secretariat by the field-leaders and the senior worker animals only. That way dangerous, progressive ideas, such as animals working at the times of day best suited to their kind, could be kept safely in check. President also needed the announcement of an initiative, such as the Working Conditions Edict, to distract the ordinary animals after one of the Secretariat was caught conducting a barter fraud where swedes had been passed off as turnips.

To Normandsky's horror (for after the deposing of Duchess, relations within the Belostrovo Animal Committee were still in a fragile state), President wanted to put the Working Conditions Edict on the agenda at the next Council meeting. Normandsky knew that this fresh set of instructions from the Co-operative would only increase the determination of that growing faction on

Belostrovo which had come to believe, after the event, that perhaps Duchess had been right all along to resist the Co-operative's encroachment into their affairs. His rival for the Chair, a goat named Windy was enthusiastic, though. The Caprine Brother declaimed at great length, how failure to adopt the Working Conditions Edict would mean a dangerous lack of valuable new rules on how to run fields, rules which no farm could do without, which wanted to think of itself as modern.

As Normandsky had a hard-enough job to get the wider Belostrovo Animal Committee to agree to a Joint Account, let alone allowing the Co-operative to take control in yet another area too, he announced his firm intention to oppose the Working Conditions Edict. At the same time, though, he agreed that he would not block the other farms joining together in a Single Account, to prove Belostrovo's good intentions towards the Co-operative.

But President was still angry, he was determined that every farm must join the Single Account, without fail, otherwise he and his eventual successors would not have full control over all the farms. He fulminated to his subordinates, 'If I have to provoke another crisis on Belostrovo, I surely will.'

But even more than Belostrovo's foot-dragging over the Working Conditions Edict, he was angry at Normandsky's misguided enthusiasm that the farms should work together jointly in new areas not previously part of the Second Annex discussions - a Co-operative Gendarmerie and a common policy for liaising with the county authorities. This latter item was an expansion of the earlier proposed common approach to competing at market with the other farms from the neighbouring counties. But as Normandsky saw it, the Gendarmerie and common external policies should not be under the control of the Co-operative's Secretariat. President derogatorily claimed that this form of co-operation, on a unanimous basis, was no better than Joint-animalism, as Abraham had named it all those years ago. Effectively, it was the same principle by which General had sought to take control of the Co-operative by pairing directly with the erstwhile West Chernopol to exclude the Secretariat.

From behind the scenes, President arranged for one of the Chairs to author a new draft of the Second Annex, addressing the additional areas identified by Normandsky. But this animal caused his anger too. Although the Working Conditions Edict had been included in the new text, and although even more of the policy areas where the Co-operative already issued edicts were now to be decided by majority voting, policing by the Gendarmerie and County liaison would remain under Joint-animalist principles. President raged that this Joint-animalism would 'pollute' the Pan-animalist nature of the Co-operative.

When the draft was sent to the Belostrovo Animal Committee for them to debate (they only got to read it by accident, thanks to a mistake by an apprentice at the printers in Vilagrad), one of Normandsky's allies got up to speak. He tried to explain the difference between Pan- and Joint-animalism, but the nuance was lost on the Animal Committee. Of late, whenever Normandsky or his rival spoke at barn meetings on matters relating to the Co-operative, the sheep had simply taken to bleating 'Co-operative good, Belostrovo bad.' For the Animal Committee members, listening to the chants of the sheep was easier than having to think too deeply on items such as new annexes. They were finding that thinking was becoming more and more difficult these days anyway, given that whole areas which they had used to debate, such as the harvest schedule, were now directed by the Co-operative for reasons of Quality Control. This troubled some of the Committee members who had enjoyed working together in the past to solve Belostrovo's problems, but now spent their time deciding only matters of lesser import (that is, when they were not excused from Committee duties, which also seemed to happen more and more these days). But on reading the draft annex, the faction which suspected that Duchess might have been right, now began to harden and set their faces against any further transfer of powers to the Co-operative. Just as it seemed that Normandsky was going to have his very own Animal Riot to deal with, he had a reprieve from a completely unexpected direction - the new rebellion on Krasnaya Farm.

Following Krasnaya Farm's insolvency, the animals had separated into groups who fended for themselves, breaking up the farm into smaller parcels of fields. One faction of the younger pigs, not closely associated with the former leadership, took control of the windmill at a knockdown price, mysteriously producing a bag of golden rubles right at the very end of the bankruptcy auction. Another group of animals, on the western border with Chernopol, took over the grain silo and its surrounding fields, then promptly fell out with each other. President, Jet and Tonton were privately delighted at this development. It was a chance to prove that the Co-operative could have influence outside the boundaries of its constituent farms, by bringing the dispute (right on its doorstep, so to speak) to an end without the intervention of the police constable at Vilagrad. The triumvirate's first thought was to preserve the unity of Krasnaya Farm, as it made no sense to them why the animals might want to direct their own affairs, free from the pigs. After all, just like the triumvirate themselves, the pigs were also higher animals.

A delegation from the Co-operative was accordingly sent to the farmhouse on Krasnaya Farm to speak with the pigs and encourage them to keep the property intact, by telling them that the Co-operative would refuse to have any dealings with the new farms which had split off. Somewhat embarrassingly for the delegation, earlier that day, as they made their way past the grain silo, they had seen it decked with the Co-operative's green flag. This was an act of solidarity by the rebel animals with the triumvirate's representatives, whom they thought would support them against the pigs. But after dinner at the farmhouse that evening, the leader of the Co-operative animals caused disappointment by making a toast to the pigs and to the unity of the farm. The very next day, though, the delegation changed its mind, when they realised that the pigs were actually quite happy for the rebels to fight amongst themselves, if the porkers could retain the farm's most valuable assets. On the delegation's return, the Co-operative acknowledged the rights of the separatists, claiming (without irony) that farms could not, after all, be forced together.

As the weeks passed, despite further delegations, conferences and proclamations, the Co-operative was not able to prevent a single stone being thrown or a single straw bale being set alight, and Krasnaya Farm remained divided into its parts. Eventually, after all this activity, it still fell to the constable from Vilagrad to cycle over and tell the rebels to take down the Green Flag and make their peace with one other. The verdict of the Chairs on the performance of the leader of the delegation was damning. One said the whole episode had merely proved the Co-operative to be a 'commercial giant, a political pygmy, but a military larva'.

Much chastened, President returned to the text of the Second Annex. His new approach recognised that to establish a Single Account, he could not force all the farms to join, but could only commence with those constituents who were willing. A Co-operative Gendarmerie and the County liaison policy would also have to be run under Joint-animalist principles for the time being, as the Chairs had wished. But if he could not have these areas decided by majority voting, he planned to pull into the Co-operative's domain as many other areas of farm administration as he was able. Just as he eventually planned for the Gendarmerie, he knew it would only be a matter of time before these areas also migrated to the control of the

Pan-animalist Secretariat in a future annex.

To make his temper even shorter, the Barleyfield office (now a dramatic five storeys tall, higher than any other farm building in the county, apart from Krasnaya Farm's windmill) was found to have dry rot and had to be completely evacuated. This was why the annex negotiations concluded at the smaller, secondary office compound on the newly renamed Chernopol, whose Animal Committee had moved out from there, back into the original farmhouse on the former East Chernopol. In a foul mood and with bitter anti-Belostrovo sentiments, President riled the crowd which had assembled on the banks of Chernopol Brook to watch the arrival of their leaders to decide their future.

Normandsky was faced with a difficult dilemma - he was damned, whatever he agreed, to divide his supporters on the Animal Committee, who were becoming ever more vociferous in their opinions on both the Single Account and the Working Conditions Edict. At least he knew that on the question of a Co-operative Militia (this suggestion kept popping up, seemingly from nowhere, every couple of years), he would have support from his Animal Committee to say 'no' and did so gladly. Although Krasnaya Farm was no longer a threat, and East Chernopol had been absorbed back into Chernopol, the need for the Co-operative to have its own Militia was apparently even more important than ever. But he wanted to be supportive of the other Chairs' plans for the next stage, so happily said 'yes', on a Joint-animalist basis, to the creation of the Co-operative Gendarmerie, intended to one day have powers to make arrests on any farm, for any crime.

But President wanted more, he wanted to at least try to get Belostrovo to agree to participate in the Single Account when the Second Annex was signed, fearful that if they did not agree now, they never would. To force consensus on all the outstanding issues, but especially to undermine

Normandsky's opposition to joining the Single Account, refreshment in the Council meeting was refused to speed up the talks. At two in the morning, a solution was found. Belostrovo would sign up to the full annex (now without mention of the Single Account), but a secondary, side annex would be signed whereby every other farm would join the Single Account, using the 'institutions' of the Co-operative to implement it.

The new annex provided for many unexpected benefits, not previously discussed in detail. Finally, as desired by Albert at the time of the First Annex, every animal on every farm would now become a citizen of the 'County Farmers' Combine' (as the Co-operative was to be renamed) whether they wanted to be or not. Why any farm, yet alone a collection of farms needed 'citizens' was not clear, neither was the reason for the plan by the Co-operative to issue internal passports stamped with the Green Flag in one corner (perhaps the animals would need these to work on other farms). As a final inducement, the Equipment Fund was to be replaced with a 'Friendship Fund', to ensure the animals knew that the new Combine would be a friendly concern.

Majority voting was extended to many unexpected new areas too, such as districtisation, whereby each farm had to report its crop output to the Co-operative by sub-groups of fields. Normandsky suspected this was to break up the sense of the old-fashioned farm boundaries, replacing them with ones approved by the Co-operative. But that was not all the Second Annex contained. It also called for the Co-operative to commence initiatives in areas such as: animal health, the supply of firewood, practical instruction of the lower animals, a telegraph system, the promotion of 'culture', building regulations, and a thing called the 'Trans-Combine Network'. This was to be a set of farm lanes connecting up the new districts directly with one another, bypassing the farmhouses where the tracks presently converged.

During the all-night discussion, a new concept called 'Animalist Delegationism' had also been introduced, between the fourth and fifth course at dinner. This concept had the highly attractive characteristic of meaning whatever any animal wished it to. In the case of President and Normandsky, this was often exactly the opposite at the same time. Under this principle, the Co-operative agreed it could intervene in areas where it was not explicitly allowed to, if it was decided this was in the best interests of the Co-operative. As far as Normandsky was concerned, Animalist Delegationism meant individual farms would run their affairs, in those few areas still left to them, without the interference of the Co-operative.

In the grey morning light, as the animals returned to the conference table to sign the Second Annex, typed up overnight by relays of ducks, it became apparent that it was very long in its final form and filled with arcane references to other documents. This had the advantage, as far as President was concerned, that no animal, especially Normandsky, could be sure just what they were signing up to. Relieved that his ordeal in front of President was over, Normandsky returned later that day to Belostrovo in triumph, greeting his supporters at the gate to the farm and showing them the notice from the Co-operative of the signing of the annex, which was to be posted on the barn wall. 'This is a piece of paper for our time,' he proclaimed, his long grey face serious on the outside, as only a donkey's can be.

At the next barn meeting, he called upon the Belostrovo Animal Committee to pass a motion, praising his achievement, which they did with some enthusiasm. Certain animals (again, typically the former supporters of Duchess) somewhat spoiled the mood by asking to see the text of the annex he had just signed, and that they were now being asked to ratify. Normandsky's answer was for them to go to the Co-operative's library at the Barleyfield office, just as soon as the dry rot had been cured.

There was criticism from another side too. Windy was upset that the Working Conditions Edict had not been signed up to and claimed that Belostrovo was a horse-drawn farm in a new world of steam tractors, the first of which had been seen on Chernopol the previous year. Normandsky's response was that the ordinary animals were simply uninterested in Windy's tedious and lengthy points of detail, and that it would be wrong to cause distress by allowing them to see the higher animals arguing over whether the annex was a good or a bad thing. In any case, he argued, Animalist Delegationism proved he had been successful in establishing the principle that the first steps away from centralised control by the Co-operative might one day be taken.

Despite the grumbles, it seemed like the debate was going Normandsky's way, and he would soon be able to get the Belostrovo Animal Committee to approve the annex. Then came the intervention of Datchanina Farm, one of the smaller constituents of the Co-operative, a highly efficient dairy operation, whose cows produced more milk per head than those on the other farms. The Animal Committee there had made the fatal mistake of giving each animal a copy of the full Second Annex, whether they could read it or not. Even for those who could read, the text was incomprehensible, so the animals took the practical view that if they could not understand it, their Animal Committee probably could not either. When ratification was put to a Vote of Confidence at their barn meeting, the Second Annex was rejected. The Chairs at the other farms were outraged that Datchanina Farm had even asked the ordinary animals the question in the first place and insisted that it be put back to them, because they clearly did not understand what they had voted on. In a pure spirit of Pan-animalism, it was made very clear to the Datchanina Chair, that the farm would correct its error, however many votes it might take. When asked why he had confidence in such an outcome, one of the members of the Secretariat claimed that, 'only donkeys do not change their minds', in a backhanded insult to Normandsky.

Despite this setback, Tonton decided that he would have to give the Frantsiya Farm animals a Vote of Confidence on the annex too. Given their love of protest and free expression he knew they would not want to miss out on the opportunity to build a festal barricade. Now, Tonton, in turn, was grateful for the discovery of Animalist Delegationism and its almost infinite elasticity. He claimed to the animals that Delegationism was actually a provision in the Second Annex which gave special permission for Frantsiya Farm to ignore any edicts they disagreed with. All the other Chairs praised the concept too, claiming that to oppose Animalist Delegationism would be like supporting the idea that a fox should have a free run of the hen-house.

To Tonton's immense relief, but to Normandsky's growing dread, Frantsiya Farm voted to approve the new annex. Normandsky was coming around to the view that it was more trouble than it was worth and had been secretly hoping Frantsiya Farm would reject it, to give him an excuse to do so too. His unease was because the supporters of the former Chair, Duchess, were now vowing to block the ratification of the entire annex at Animal Committee. Normandsky complained that the Animal Committee had praised his achievement in signing the annex and was annoyed that now that the animals had finally read it, they did not like it.

Normandsky gave an impassioned speech, referring to Animalist Delegationism seventy-one times. He insisted it meant that after the Second Annex was ratified, Belostrovo would carry on as it had done before - that the gentle shadows over its fields, warm mash, tidy rows of hen-houses and the traditional frolics of the dogs would not be in danger from a Combine. The final vote was close, won by a mere three votes, thanks to a combination of threats and the strange, unexpected defection to Normandsky's side of a group of eight ducks, who represented the fields on the other side of the fishing lake. But the lasting result was that his faction at Committee was even more bitterly divided than ever.

Now the only remaining obstacle to the Second Annex was once again Datchanina Farm. President's plan was that the Chair would 'declare' that Co-operative citizenship would not mean that the animals must stop calling Datchanina Farm their home, that their farm would have to join the Single Account or that their younger animals would be compelled to serve time in the new Co-operative Gendarmerie. The fact that none of these things were actually present in the Second Annex was irrelevant, all that mattered was that their Chair had given the impression he had negotiated with President to remove them. Despite this theatre, only just enough of the animals were convinced to approve the Annex at the second time of asking. Others, continuing to be suspicious of their leader, barricaded off part of the farmyard in protest, declaring it a 'Co-operative-free zone', until the dogs chased them off.

President claimed that the ruckus on Datchanina Farm was proof that, left to themselves, the lesser animals would certainly revert to wildness, just as Abraham had used to warn his acolytes about. So, in celebration of the ratification of Second Annex, President came up with a new slogan using the Co-operative's new name, for the Chairs to post up around their farms: 'The Combine Protects Us From Ourselves.'

Chapter VIII - Глава VIII

The Combine now started its work in earnest. The dry rot infested Barleyfield office was gutted and rebuilt with an extra, sixth, storey on top, and a second wing added too, allowing the number of animal officials to be doubled. And they had a lot to do. New edicts were issued in the areas added under the terms of the Second Annex and animals were docked rations for using the incorrect tools or storing produce in containers of non-standard measurement. What had not changed was the process by which new edicts were decided upon, which remained somewhat opaque. Often, a concerned group of animals would put forward ideas directly to the Secretariat, who would then negotiate details with officials at the individual farms before taking the completed edicts up to the Council for them to send back down to the Secretariat. So many edicts were being written, that the Chairs did not have time to read them all before agreeing to them (which they always did). In fact, the Chairs' own secretaries would simply mark the lists before each meeting to identify the edicts which were specifically not to be discussed at Council (which was most of them).

Once the edicts had been issued by the Combine, it was up to each farm to promulgate them, following their own procedures. At Chernopol, each edict was tested against the farm's own constitution and at Frantsiya Farm the edicts were filed haphazardly in a large and dusty cupboard in the corner of their office. At Belostrovo the Animal Committee felt it was beneath their dignity to continue to transcribe edicts from the Combine onto headed notepaper, as they had been used to. This task was now given to a new class of officials, specially employed to administer the ever-growing number of regulations (the source edicts now filled three cabinets placed high up in the attic of the farmhouse, balanced on the rafters). These officials took great pride in faithfully copying across the rules, and often tried to divine what the Combine had really meant when writing them. Often, they would add extra codicils to underline their personal loyalty to the Combine by interpreting its edicts in the strictest way possible. For example, if the previous policy had been to require the composting of red onion tops and beetroot stalks together, but the new edict added radishes to the list, then the subsequent Belostrovo regulation would include rhubarb as well, just in case the Combine had meant the edict to include all red plants. The Animal Committee was happy for its officials to transcribe the edicts, to fetch Korolsky's signature stamp block from the farm accountant's desk before Committee meetings, and sometimes even to stamp regulations of lesser importance on the Committee's behalf, such those promulgated on county liaison issues.

But the need for all these new edicts was becoming difficult to explain to the Combine's animals, and Datchanina Farm was often in President's mind. To create a more emotional bond between the Combine and its citizens, he instructed that the word 'combine' should be replaced in conversation with 'county' wherever possible. His advisors came up with new slogans, such as 'Together for the County for the Benefit of Us All', and 'Mother County Must Protect Her Children.' It was even suggested a special campaign should be mounted to promote President to female animals. Together with the sloganeering, it was decided a new, more interesting and attractive history of the farms was needed, one which emphasised the central role of the Combine in the events of the past. The principle story told, known to every animal from the time they were chick or pup, was that it had been the Combine which had settled the boundary dispute over the water-meadow between Klemansky and Nemetsky. It had also been the Combine which had liberated the fishing lake of Belostrovo for the use of all animals, and it had been the Combine which had caused the peaceful removal of the Fence, uniting Chernopol once again.

Despite the flood of edicts, the farms did not seem to be that much more prosperous than before. Chernopol still did well but was not getting wealthier at the same pace as in its early years. Having to pay, virtually for the complete rebuilding of the former East Chernopol was a burden, albeit one the western Chernopol animals had been happy to bear. The answer to the prosperity question, as far as President was concerned, was to push for more powers to be transferred to the Combine in a Third Annex, and he was about to be given a new excuse to do so.

Meanwhile, the Combine's Council meetings were becoming more and more surreal. Given the detailed negotiations which always preceded each meeting, there seemed little point in lengthy debate at Council - especially as it was invariably the combined wishes of Frantsiya Farm and Chernopol which carried the day. The other constituents grumbled but fell strangely silent when additional Equal Rations or increased investment by the Friendship Fund were promised to them. Dissent at the Council from the common line was considered a gross offence against Pan-animalism and therefore verging on Wildness.

President's opportunity to acquire more powers via a Third Annex came from the western parts of Krasnaya Farm, which now asked to join the Combine. The animals there had had enough of the chaos of bankruptcy and had been seduced by the promises of Equal Rations. President planned to increase majority voting in all existing areas, and also appoint an actual Combine liaison officer, not simply to have a common liaison policy. He also decided that the Combine would decide the policy for all farms regarding the settlement of new animals arriving from outside the county. The Combine's Gendarmerie would gain extra powers, although the Gendarmerie would remain for now under Joint-animalist principles.

Although, at the start of discussions, it seemed that the Third Annex would only make incremental changes, Normandsky at Belostrovo realised that adding new farms would mean more animals voting at the Council meetings to authorise the edicts presented by the Secretariat. He feared that this increase would mean that Belostrovo would be outvoted on an even more regular occurrence than happened at present and would perhaps even be forced to join the Single Account one day. He begged President not to link the expansion of the Combine to the extension of majority voting, reminding him of the principle of Animalist Delegationism with which he had tricked the Belostrovo Animal Committee into approving the Second Annex. In the end, President agreed that a Chair would be able to vote against new edicts, but only with the effect of causing a 'very short delay.' Even Normandsky could no longer pretend that Animalist Delegationism was making any difference, much to the derision of his opponents on the Animal Committee.

Jet had reflected on President's progress and likewise come to the conclusion that there was not support for a large package of new powers for the Combine - his preference was now on advancing the ongoing preparation for the Single Account, agreed under the Second Annex, because Chernopol would effectively run it.

Jet's clear support to make the Single Account a reality sent the concept's supporters at Belostrovo into a frenzy. They commissioned surveys which showed that eighty-two percent of large animals favoured the Single Account, and that fifty-five percent of hens thought that joining the Single Account was necessary for them to be able to carry on laying eggs. The supporters were panicked that Belostrovo would be left out of any moves towards a fully-unified farm, claiming that its status had still not fully recovered from the water rights lawsuit (although they were hard-pressed to find many animals who remembered even the story of that event). Despite these intelligent and persuasive arguments, the ordinary animals, however, remained stubbornly unconvinced. Normandsky now found, just as Duchess had, that the senior animals on the Committee were still deeply split on the issue. He was even threatened with a personal Vote of Confidence at Committee, which he won, but which undermined him further, making him look foolish in front of the ordinary animals. He tried to paper over the divisions in the Committee by supporting a meaningless Solemn Declaration issued by the Combine, praising the strength of conviction of its founders, Clefthoof and Rock. At the same time, to the ordinary animals at barn meetings, he again praised the idea of Animalist Delegationism, but without mentioning how the discussions on the proposed Third Annex had already proven it to be hollow. He carried on praising the idea at Council too, but it now had to be admitted that he, like Duchess before him, was gradually losing touch with reality - at one point he even claimed in the third person that, 'Normandsky is proving to be as popular with the animal citizens of the Combine as Jet.'

Back at Belostrovo, the artificial enthusiasm which had been whipped up for the Single Account could not be sustained. For the first time since Belostrovo had voted to stay in the County Farmers' Co-operative, all factions within the Animal Committee claimed they would put the question of joining the Single Account, if it was ever forced on Belostrovo, to another farm-wide Vote of Confidence. Promising this was preferable to having to make a clear decision on joining or to committing to a date for the same. Then came two further distractions to help

Belostrovo forget about the Single Account for a while, and to further chill their attitude towards the Combine.

One of the other constituent farms, High Spring Farm, had taken up fishing with enthusiasm after their Animal Riot, which had taken place somewhat later than on the other farms. Like Chernopol, they had started fishing from a stream, which flowed out from a spring under the high escarpment overlooking the farm, giving it its name. The High Spring animals took to fishing with such enjoyment, that they began to roam the county, surreptitiously casting their lines wherever they found an unwatched pond. So, when they joined the Co-operative (as it then was), they started fishing in Belostrovo's lake with glee. Soon, of a weekend, the banks would be positively crowded with High Spring animals. In fact, they not only used up all their own licences (issued to them by the Combine) but could sometimes be seen bartering mangel-wurzels for licenses issued to Belostrovo animals too. Eventually, the High Spring animals had fished Belostrovo's lake so enthusiastically, that stocks began to be seriously depleted. The Fishing License committee at Belostrovo could no longer turn a blind eye and one day confiscated a rod from a High Spring animal who every Saturday morning sat there, quite unashamed, with two poles on stands, waiting for a bite. In protest, this animal complained to the Combine, who pronounced that he had just as much right to take fish caught with a Belostrovo license as any Belostrovo animal and ordered the farm to pay him forty kopeks in compensation. This did not make the Combine any more popular at Belostrovo, especially after what came next.

One morning, the Quality Control inspector noted wilting leaves on some of the plants in the mangel-wurzel field. On closer inspection, it was decided this was not due to the unseasonably hot weather, but instead to a new, as yet unidentified disease, which the inspector decided to name Mangel-wurzel Atrophy Disease. The Combine placed an immediate ban on the transport of Belostrovo's mangel-wurzels to the other farms, and indeed, demanded that Belostrovo uproot the entire field on animal health grounds. Normandsky pointed out that this would drive up the value of mangel-wurzels across the entire Combine, and that Belostrovo would have to barter for its whole supply from the other farms, even though only a few plants were affected by the disease. President praised Normandsky for his perception, and his newly-found pro-Combine sentiments, explaining to the donkey that Belostrovo would be benefiting the entire Combine by his action. He went on to explain that in turn, the Combine, by its edict to destroy the plants, was keeping the animals of Belostrovo safe from infected mangel-wurzels. Normandsky pleaded for an amelioration of the terms of the edict, especially as he feared that his own inspectors, if unchecked, would add turnips to the list too. But the Combine was adamant, one of the Chairs insisting that if Belostrovo did not want to respect the decision of the Combine, it should leave.

As Normandsky became less and less popular, his weakness in the face of President was ever clearer to all at Belostrovo to see. The Combine's Secretary simply decided to wait until after the next Belostrovo barn meeting before signing the Third Annex, as it was certain the new leader would be a young, upcoming pig called Scratcher. As President himself said, 'Why should we change the annex for this Chair, when we simply need to wait until another animal takes his place?' However, just to make sure Normandsky would lose the election, President added the Working Conditions Edict to the final draft of the new Annex. Normandsky had consistently said there was no real benefit from this edict, so was obliged to oppose it. As planned by President, this made Normandsky look mule-headed in front of the sheep, who once more took up bleating, even more loudly, 'Combine good, Belostrovo bad,' whenever they saw him.

Despite the chaos in the Belostrovo Animal Committee, and the fishing dispute, and the diseased mangel-wurzels, overall, Belostrovo was becoming and more prosperous each year and at a faster rate than the other farms. Why this was so, was not immediately clear, perhaps running its own bank account, and being able to invest where it wanted to, had something to do with it. Maybe the animals' confidence had simply grown over time and their farm's income with it. But now they had had enough of the dull Normandsky, who represented, in their minds, a mediocre continuation of the severe rule of Duchess, such as they could remember it.

As predicted, Scratcher easily carried the barn meeting and was installed as Chair on a wave of enthusiasm. Believing in himself, in a way which Normandsky had never done in his moments of lucidity, Scratcher even went on a tour of the other farms before the next Council meeting, so he could explain to the Chairs what they were doing wrong in the management of their farms. He had even devised a new theory of farm management, which he called 'Tertiary Deviationism', acknowledging that it owed something to the early liberal thinkers of Animal Rule. Having given President instruction in Tertiary Deviationism too, he now promised the donkey that he, Scratcher, would now take the reform of the Combine in hand, delivering the change that President could not. President remained impassive at this pronouncement, after all, dissimulation was one of Abraham's cardinal principles, passed down from Secretary to Secretary.

After lengthy further discussion the Third Annex was almost ready. Scratcher had immediately agreed to the full unaltered text, including the Working Conditions Edict, proudly claiming that this proved his pro-Combine credentials. The annex was only meant to prepare for the inclusion of the breakaway parts of the old Krasnaya Farm into the Combine by further reducing veto rights in its existing areas of responsibility, but, as always, the completed document covered new, unexpected powers. The Gendarmerie were given a longer list of rule infractions they could make arrests for, and the County Liaison policy (still run for now under Joint-Animalist principles) was expanded to include making suggestions to the railway company on the timetable of trains from Vilagrad. In the week before signing, a further delay was caused by President adding extra non-binding sub-annexes to the Annex which provided for: equal working hours for male and female animals, further research into Mangelwurzel Atrophy Disease, and the freedom for any animal to live on any farm (which caused Chernopol some unease because of their generous rations). But President's favourite side-project was the design of the new bank books for the Single Account, which had images of well-known field gates from each of the farms embossed on the front. The words of 'On the Vilagrad Steppe', though, still could not be agreed upon, but that dispute would be as nothing compared to what came next.

After the Third Annex was signed, President's work was done. He had steered the Combine, from the First Annex which had introduced Common Bartering, through the episode of Duchess's removal, the Second Annex and the fall of Normandsky, all the way to the Third Annex and the imminent eastward expansion of the Combine. He had overseen the building of two additional storeys at the Barleyfield and a second wing too, providing much-deserved employment for those higher animals called to the cause of Pan-animalism. But now it was time to pass the baton on, to another donkey he had chosen (a complete coincidence that this should be so), an animal named 'Muddy', whom he had been training for many years to think and act just as he did.

Chapter IX - Глава IX

The time had almost arrived for the new farms which had broken away from Krasnaya Farm to join the Combine. The Third Annex had prepared the way by ensuring they would not have any real voting power by removing as many veto rights from the farms beforehand, as President had felt he could get away with. But now his successor, Muddy, decided that to be on the safe side he needed a Fourth Annex where the proposed voting weights of the new constituents would be calculated again (probably downwards) and that the Combine should be given a few extra powers, in thirty-nine new areas. He also announced that the practice of adding new Annexes to the constitution would end with the Fourth, and that the old constitution and its annexes would eventually be replaced with a new Constitution. This would streamline the administration of the Combine by enshrining the right of the Secretariat to take further powers from the farms without asking them.

But the Combine was clearly at a kind of crossroads – the addition of new constituents, almost as many as the existing farms, would mean that Frantsiya Farm and Chernopol required a new way of running the Combine together. Into this struggle for supremacy also came the Secretariat, whose Secretary was a kind of Animal Committee Chair in his own right, even if the actual Chairs did not fully recognise it yet. But the real question, which no one wanted to think too deeply on, was - what was the Combine's ultimate destination?

Even as the Fourth Annex was being signed, a new

argument started over Equal Rations. The largest of the prospective new constituents, Pollard Farm, was almost as large as High Spring, and had many more animals than at first thought, requiring foodstuffs which could not be grown or fished on their own farm. Chernopol, the next nearest farm to Pollard Farm indeed began to fear that once admitted, under Common Bartering principles, the Pollard Farm animals would simply move to Chernopol to earn their rations there. Frantsiya Farm's fear was rather that under the current arrangements, the animals from the east would be given the exactly the same quantities of Equal Rations as on the other farms. To placate the two western farms, the Combine proposed that in future, there would be an upper limit on the quantity of Equal Rations available to those farms with the fewest qualifying animals, which would particularly affect Belostrovo. Belostrovo would also be hit by changes to the Friendship Fund which from now on would be directed towards the poorer farms and to Frantsiya Farm.

The Animal Committee on Belostrovo did not seem to be particularly bothered about these proposals. Instead, their attention was still being consumed by the question of whether to join the Single Account. Scratcher was of the opinion that it was only a question of 'when', because, as he said with a wide grin, 'join we will.' But the Belostrovo farm accountant, a solemn cart-horse named Angus, and one-time rival of Scratcher for the Chair, disagreed. Angus claimed, that as he was in charge of the farm's finances, he should be the one to decide this question. To this end, he produced a set of five tests which would have to be met before he would recommend that Belostrovo join the Single Account. This list he usually kept hidden under the straw in his stall, but one day, whether by accident or design, he showed it to one of his associates, who reported that it simply read five times over: 'Not as long as Scratcher draws breath.' Such was the bitterness between the pig and the horse. But the farms who had joined the

Single Account were also having problems of their own. Now that they had handed control of their finances over to a representative of the Secretariat, they found that he held a tight rein (figuratively speaking, of course, for reins had been abolished at the time of the Animal Riots). Spending which previously would have been quickly agreed to, such as replacement parts for the thresher or investment in horse-drawn binders was no longer allowed. This caused friction for a few months until Frantsiya Farm and Chernopol solved the problem by telling the Combine's accountant to apply less strict spending rules to them than to the other farms.

At the next Council meeting, Scratcher proclaimed that Belostrovo would soon play a full part in the Combine when it joined the Single Account, and that he should thus join their separate agenda item discussions on the Account to give them the benefit of his instruction (again) on Tertiary Deviationism. But Jet rebuffed Scratcher, saying that his talk of applying Tertiary Deviationist principles to the Single Account had insulted the Frantsiya Farm delegation, and that he should leave the Council early when that item came up. This was Jet's valuable instruction to Scratcher, showing him how many allies he really had at the Combine's Council. Just to make sure that the pig got the point, the Secretariat decided that to conserve fish stocks in Belostrovo lake, the Animal Committee there would be required cancel half the licenses held by Belostrovo animals (but none of those which had been bartered for mangel-wurzels by High Spring).

The Secretariat began to exercise its hidden powers in the other areas given over to it by the First, Second, Third and Fourth Annexes too. As intended, each animal had finally been issued with an internal passport, with the golden hooves on green field device of the Combine. The Belostrovo Animal Committee sought to reassure their animals, fond of their own farm's historic symbols, that the design of this document had been approved by 'responsible animals' – but did not say that these responsible animals were in fact the Combine's Secretariat. In addition, under the principles of districtisation, the Secretariat now required that each farm be formally split into sub-units, each with its own Animal Sub-Committee. On Belostrovo this initiative ran into difficulty, with the animals posing simplistic questions such as 'why do we need new Committees to discuss the items on which the Belostrovo Committee have already been instructed by the Combine?' This merely proved that these animals were incapable of the complex thoughts demanded of them by membership of the Combine, so the exercise was halted, for their sake, in case they became further confused.

Following this setback, it was decided it would be a good idea to completely avoid raising any questions about the purpose of the Combine with the lower animals (even though Scratcher had told them on many occasions that the benefits it brought were what he called 'self-evident'). This silence was especially necessary, after one of the Secretariat was found to have obtained three-hundred and thirty-six portions of Equal Rations under false pretences, which he had hoped to trade for tobacco in Vilagrad. The animal who discovered this fraud was roundly punished for having brought the Combine into disrepute with his 'intolerable insinuations'. However, when a further seven hundred and two dog biscuits were found hidden in a well on Frantsiya Farm, Muddy eventually resigned his position with bad grace, before being reappointed ten minutes later as a 'caretaker' Secretary. Unfortunately, for those animals who cared about such things, Muddy interpreted 'caretaker' as meaning 'taking care' not to get caught again, which meant that the dispute quickly blew over.

As soon as the crisis of reputation had passed, the time was judged right to start explaining the need for a replacement Constitution. Muddy made an announcement, flanked by the other members of the Secretariat (including the thief) that, 'The animals of the Combine need clear answers to the very important problems of their lives,' he said. 'My Animal Committee will address the needs of all animals, even the cows of Datchanina Farm. Today we solve the problems of the Combine, tomorrow the County,' announcing that an Extraordinary General Meeting would now be called to draft the Constitution. Before that, though, apparently yet another new committee had to be created, to draw up an agenda for the 'convention', as the Extraordinary General Meeting was to be known. The Agenda Committee would also study possible forms of a constitution and would be chaired by Muddy himself. It got straight to work. The first page of the draft called for consideration of the immediate incorporation of the Gendarmerie and the County Liaison policy, currently run on Joint-animalist principles, under the full control of the Secretariat. For the benefit of Belostrovo, a clause was proposed whereby farms not taking part in the Single Account would be allowed to increase their payments into Combine funds, but otherwise could stay as they were and be ignored whilst the other farms decided which powers the Combine should take over from the farms next.

While good progress was being made, Muddy now feared that the constitutional drafting exercise would still take too long for the prospective constituents from Krasnaya Farm. They had been told they had to wait on the signing of the new Constitution before joining but soon might cool on the idea and start to think they could stand on their own feet. Scratcher started to panic too, under his carefully-brushed shiny coat, at the prospect of a deluge of new edicts which a new constitution would surely entail - so had a series of posters put up around Belostrovo extolling the benefits of the Combine. His case was not helped when the mangel-wurzel ban was finally lifted, but then promptly ignored by Chernopol and Frantsiya Farm, the latter organising a bonfire of Belostrovo roots which the farm had foolishly sent to be exchanged for rye grain. So he had yet more posters pasted on the walls of the farmhouse, listing the powers which he assured the animals the Belostrovo Animal Committee would keep after it signed the new Constitution (albeit this text not being yet available to read, even in draft). Along with this incentive, other posters claimed that one third of the animals would starve to death if Belostrovo left the Combine and that a further third would need to go into exile, to reduce the population to a level which the outcast farm could sustain. This approach was completely at odds with the other farms in the Combine where the Chairs were explaining how much better the Combine could run their farms than they or their Animal Committees ever could. To make Scratcher's task even more difficult, new noises from the drafting committee concerning the establishment of a Combine Militia were now heard. Muddy's advice to the proposers was that whatever happened, they must not use the word 'militia' – 'call it Margaret or Mariya-Anna for all I care,' he said.

But now questions on the dilution of the votes of the larger western farms, following the entry of the new farms from the east, began to be raised more sharply, as the time of their joining approached. The Chair of Frantsiya Farm began to speculate if, in fact, the pace was too fast after all. The response of Muddy was to say that the traditional leaders of the Combine, Frantsiya Farm and Chernopol should therefore help accelerate agreement on the Constitution before those other farms joined, just as General had sought to complete the agreement on Equal Rations before the entry of Belostrovo. But Frantsiya Farm's response was not what Muddy had expected. Before the committee could report, it came out with a suggestion of its own, that Frantsiya Farm and Chernopol should form a special group to agree deeper power-sharing than the other farms, and in a warning to Muddy, suggested this would take place in a rival organisation to the Combine unless Frantsiya Farm got its way.

Now it was Chernopol's turn to put forward their case in the absence of a draft constitution. The Chair of Chernopol had become frustrated by the constant ratcheting up of the powers of the Secretariat without any real disclosure on where it might end. To Scratcher's horror, the Chair now sought to set out Chernopol's clear view of that destination, blandly proposing the full amalgamation of all the farms into a single production unit. Instead of Muddy's fellow Pan-animalist appointees, he proposed the Secretariat would be elected every year, just like the Animal Committees of the constituent farms.

Scratcher tried to gloss over this vision for the benefit of the Belostrovo animals, praising what he called the 'joint plan' between Frantsiya Farm and Chernopol, completely failing to understand the vast difference between what each was calling for. He steadfastly claimed, that no matter how the Combine developed, it was Belostrovo's destiny to be a leading constituent.

Muddy's reaction was to be expected, though – he quietly dismissed the idea of a unified farm with an elected Secretariat as being too open to the influence of lower animals. He dismissed too, Frantsiya Farm's alternative plan of a new Combine, operating at a higher level than the County Farmers' Combine. Muddy claimed that this left his new constitution as the only logical remaining option to strengthen the existing Combine, by quickly and painlessly removing more of the farms' veto rights.

To satisfy the larger farms' impatience, he made the Agenda Committee publish its preliminary draft for the convention, which now included a statement of all the 'rights' of the Combine's animals. A sub-paragraph, however, noted that 'any right can be removed if deemed necessary to meet the objectives of general interest being pursued by the Combine.' This gave Muddy great reassurance when he saw it, as it would be his Secretariat who had the power to make this judgment.

In the meantime, to spoil his mood, at that point

Datchanina Farm held another farm-wide Vote of Confidence on whether to join the Single Account after all, which the animals promptly rejected. This was despite Muddy's stern injunction to the Chair there not to hold such a vote again, saying it would be 'irresponsible, irrational, and foolish.' The Chair of Datchanina Farm replied that the vote had been held according to their own farm's Constitution, to which Muddy helpfully pointed out, that as this document would shortly be superfluous anyway, there had been no point in the exercise.

Annoyed as Muddy was, the mood of Scratcher was, if anything, worse – he was determined not to let the Belostrovo animals have the same kind of say, for he feared they had not been convinced by his poster campaign. Indeed, he suspected that despite his best efforts to present Belostrovo as a progressive, forward-thinking farm to the other Chairs, at home the animals had, if anything, year by year been growing more sceptical towards the Combine. With a growing sense of desperation, he went around the other farms, telling each Chair what they wanted to hear, to try to hurry along an agreement before further questions were raised on Belostrovo.

To Frantsiya Farm he claimed he agreed that a triumvirate of Frantsiya Farm, Chernopol and Belostrovo should guide and direct the choices of the other farms. At Chernopol he agreed that the Constitution needed to set out the clear definition of the new powers of the Secretariat which Chernopol had demanded. He also came up with some of his own ideas too, which sounded little different to the Animalist Delegationism which Normandsky had once championed. Then he claimed that a new constitution would make almost no difference anyway, as the Combine already had one, and as that the Combine was not a unified farm today it was preposterous to believe it would ever become one in the future. Then he excitedly went back Frantsiya Farm and proposed his triumvirate idea again. Then back to Muddy and a stronger Secretariat. By now poor Angus, who had been carefully watching Scratcher from a distance, was thoroughly confused and glowered at the pig from under his shaggy cart-horse's forelock. Scratcher completed his frantic tour with the cryptic pronouncement that he was still 'in favour of the Combine, but what sort of Combine?' But it fell to Chernopol to put him out of his misery and put Belostrovo back into its place by rejecting his final idea, a Belostrovo-Chernopol axis to give joint inspiration to the other farms.

After this rebuff and sensing himself weakened at the Council, he did the only thing which he and his predecessors knew of, to get the favour of the other farms - promising to give up Belostrovo's veto rights in yet more areas. On the renewed question of joining the Single Account Scratcher was firm though, mainly because Angus pressed down hard on his curled tail with a great cart-horse's hoof as the pig spoke at the Council.

Eventually, the Agenda Committee had finished its work, including an approximate preliminary agreement with High Spring and Pollard Farm on voting rights, and drafting of the Constitution could now start in earnest at the convention. Scratcher again confidently predicted that after the Constitution was signed, powers would actually be returned to Belostrovo, oblivious to the smirks from the other Chairs behind him.

Chapter X - Глава X

The convention started with great fanfare. Muddy made a solemn pledge that after the Constitution was agreed and signed, the Combine's work would be almost complete and that any further expansion of its powers would be unnecessary, as long as that did not interfere in the 'dynamic' of the county. On the first day the convention sat, Muddy also pronounced that there would be no vote on the final draft by the delegates, instead, Muddy himself would 'divine' where the consensus lay. With the Chairs excluded from the running of the convention, its deliberations defaulted to the Secretariat's view, which was that it should draft something to merely confirm that almost all the real day-to-day responsibility of running a farm was now in the hands of the Secretariat.

But just as the Secretariat had got the convention firmly under its control, further fraud was uncovered in the Combine's affairs. Its accountant, a mare named Mariya, refused to sign off on the books, claiming that the way its finances were run was open to gross abuse. Mariya was particularly upset at the fact that cheques were written out in pencil and that Muddy had the only key to the safe. Muddy's response was that signing off on the accounts was the only reason she had been employed by the Combine in the first place, and if any gross abuse had taken place, it was surely her abuse of the reputation of the Combine. Shortly after, to make sure she understood this point, Windy sacked her in a lengthy memo sent from his office on the top floor of the Barleyfield office. To everyone's surprise, Windy, who having been beaten by the dull Normandsky in the final election he contested, had been given a new lease of life working for the Combine. There, he was in overall charge of both the Combine's accounts and the allowances granted by the Secretariat to the Combine's Animal Committee.

While the convention continued to sit, rumblings over Belostrovo's complicated rebate on its payments into the Equal Rations plan started again. Further trouble was rumoured, too, over the refusal of Chernopol to allow Pollard Farm animals to move there to work for rations, from fear there would not be enough work for all the animals finding themselves on the farm. Then, yet another fraud was discovered, in the accounts office itself. By this time, frauds were so common that the ordinary animals had stopped concerning themselves about them, assuming they were simply part of the cost of living together in a large group, and that nothing could change.

This newly reasonable attitude bought the convention just enough time for Muddy's plan to come to fruition. So intent was he, not to give Chernopol or Frantsiya Farm any inkling of what was about to be announced, his special commission had been meeting for many months in the basement of the Barleyfield office (for it now possessed an underground level), producing a draft, so secret that it had been given a code-name: 'Penelope'. Although it appeared that much time had been wasted with the Agenda Committee which had met before the Convention, and then in the Convention's deliberations to date, the reason was now clear. 'Penelope' was presented to the convention as a fully drafted constitution, ready for immediate signature. It contained many changes from the Fourth Annex, not least the replacement of the voting system agreed under that Annex for one more favourable to Frantsiya Farm and Chernopol. The document made the legal superiority of the Secretariat's edicts to any regulation issued by a farm explicit for the first time and brought the Joint-animalist areas of the Third Annex under Combine control. It also contained a special clause, whereby the Council could escalate the Combine's power by agreeing to abolish vetoes without the need for a new Annex. Also, controversially, a legal description of the Combine was given for the first time. It would now be referred to in contracts as a 'farm' – despite it not owning any fields of its own. The Council was to have its own permanent Secretary too, and there would be an actual County Liaison Officer, employed by the Secretariat, to be the Combine's representative for its external policies. To the answer the objection of Belostrovo to the use of the word 'united' when describing the characteristics of this new combine, it was replaced in the text with 'amalgamated'. All in all, the new draft was actually longer, by some two-fifths, than the old constitution and annexes it replaced.

Although the Combine was now to be described as a 'farm', it was really rather more a kind of 'super Animal Committee', hidden behind the actual Animal Committees of the farms, directing their work. But the special escalator clause showed that instead of being a completed work, the new Constitution was likely merely to be yet another staging post on the journey of the Combine to acquire new powers, just as each Annex had been.

Muddy looked around the room, beaming, and said 'This is imperfect, but is more than could have been hoped for.' He then divined a consensus at the Convention in support of the document.

Now that the draft was real, the Chairs faced the harder question of ratification. Scratcher tried to claim the Constitution was only an administrative 'tidying up exercise', which simply consolidated the existing constitution and its four Annexes into a single text, saving on the costs of binding at the printers. He claimed that the escalator clause proved, in fact, that Joint-animalism and Pan-animalism had always been in harmony with each other, with one flowing seamlessly into the other. One of his allies said that the rumour that the Combine was now officially a 'farm', was a false understanding by the ordinary animals of the wording used. He explained that only higher animals could truly understand, that instead of being a farm in its own right, it was merely a collection of fields under one management.

To the Belostrovo animals, Scratcher declared that the Constitution represented a victory for their farm over the others. He claimed he had personally negotiated hard, achieving ninety-nine percent of what he felt Belostrovo needed from the convention, and that in any case, the Constitution was only 'highly desirable, not absolutely essential.' However, despite his honeyed words, still fewer animals were believing him these days. The main reason was Angus, in the presence of whose dour expression even Scratcher became distracted when speaking, only maintaining his toothy smile with difficulty. The animals were also growing suspicious that despite his continual enthusiasm for Tertiary Deviationism, he did not seem to be able to explain what it really meant, or how it would make their lives better.

Despite the Constitution not yet being ratified, the Combine immediately took steps to form a joint-stock railway company, as called for in the text. It was judged highly important for the Combine to build a new line from Vilagrad to the neighbouring county, so it would not be dependent on the existing service. The Combine also created a Quartermaster's Depot for its future Militia, also as envisaged in the Constitution. Muddy immediately sent to Vilagrad for a catalogue of shotguns, and several days later, one of the Combine's Animal Committee members came limping in from the field with pellets in its hind leg. This animal, having nothing else to do, had foolishly agreed to drag a target across the field for the donkey, who had tried to aim and shoot the gun with a complicated frame and pulley contraption.

After the initial euphoria of the publishing of the Constitution's text, it was discovered that the fraud in the

Combine's accounts office was worse than feared and suspicion was directed at Windy, who had got a taste for luxury since leaving Belostrovo. This was the somewhat subdued background to the signing of the Constitution by the Chairs at a specially convened Council meeting. Scratcher was dreading this moment, for, in a moment of foolishness, in an attempt to maintain his popularity with the Belostrovo animals he had succumbed to the madness of Datchanina Farm and promised them a Vote of Confidence in the Constitution, once he had signed it. But his agonising was exposed for the narcissism it was by the Chair of the largest of the new joining constituents, Pollard Farm, who refused outright to attend the ceremony. The Pollard Farm Chair claimed that he could not see the difference between the rule of the pigs on the old Krasnaya Farm and being forced to obey the many hundreds of new edicts produced by Secretariat every year (let alone the thousands of existing ones they had already been required to adopt, prior to joining). In reaction, the Chair of Frantsiya Farm hubristically declared that any farm refusing to ratify the Convention should quit the Combine. Pollard Farm was finally won round with a last-minute concession on voting weights at Council (even though these were becoming less valuable with each additional area where vetoes were taken away). So the Chairs duly signed the Constitution, full of arcane references to the old constitution and its annexes, without really understanding what they had agreed.

Now came the process of ratification across all the farms. Muddy sent the Chairs back to their animals with his inspirational speech ringing in their ears – 'if it is a "yes", we go on, if it is a "no", we continue.' At this, Scratcher's blood pressure rose even higher, for he felt sure that without strong coercion, his animals would not agree to the path the Combine was taking. Some of them could remember the fierce arguments of the Animal Committee over the Second Annex and had long wanted their own say on what the Combine seemed to have become in the preceding years, without them realising it.

It did not help the case for giving the Secretariat more powers, that at that moment, two of its members were caught in a new Equal Rations fraud. And by now, the complexity of the text was causing problems too, even for its own supporters who were trying to explain its benefits. On the other side, the Constitution's sceptics were especially suspicious when they worked out that the concatenation of three separate clauses in two different parts of the document gave the Secretariat (not just the Council using the 'escalator' clause) the right to remove veto powers in yet more areas. Muddy did have some early good news, though, when to his delight, a rival co-operative in the neighbouring county, run entirely by pigs, praised the Constitution as being 'undoubtedly the work of a genius with extraordinary skills.'

But the Frantsiya Farm animals obviously did not agree with that pronouncement. In an earthquake which shook the Combine to its very foundations, the farm which had benefited the most from it over the years rejected the Constitution in their Vote of Confidence. The only saving grace, as far as Muddy was concerned, was that this rejection came about partly because the animals had had enough of their own Chair's corruption. The removal of problem Chairs was something the Combine had become expert at over the years, so Muddy was not overly concerned. In the case of Frantsiya Farm's Chair this was even less so – it was an open-and-shut case of him having been caught taking bribes from the printer at Vilagrad for the supply of the textbooks used to teach the younger animals the principles of Pan-animalism.

To distract from the disaster and to shore up the remaining support on Frantsiya Farm for the Combine, the Chair immediately called for the recalculation of Belostrovo's contribution to Equal Rations from the sales levy, in favour of his farm. A former ally of Scratcher, dismissed from Belostrovo on suspicions of fraud there, had turned up at the Barleyfield office to be employed by the Secretariat for his special skills, overseeing the Equal Rations plan for the Combine. This saturnine creature now declared that Belostrovo should demonstrate 'greater fairness' to Frantsiya Farm's demand for more Equal Rations per head for its animals. The sly animal claimed that despite Equal Rations having been one of Abraham's earliest initiatives, the arrangement still represented 'a modern and dynamic policy that conformed to the interests of the Combine.'

In Datchanina Farm, the admonished Animal Committee took no chances. To help the slow-of-thought ordinary animals understand why they should support the Constitution, the Animal Committee put up posters of wolves and bears with the slogan 'The Combine Saves Us From Falling Back Into Wildness'. Clever as this campaign was, it fell foul of the lack of imagination of the lower animals. A duck exclaimed upon seeing one of the posters, that, 'ducks have never had claws, as far back as ducks can remember,' and did not see why this would change, whether the farm was part of the Combine or not. Unsurprisingly, despite their Animal Committee's best efforts, Datchanina Farm rejected the Constitution. Although Muddy had suspected this might happen, his reaction was still one of anger, claiming that Datchanina Farm had voted against the Constitution, without realising it was actually, 'the answer to the questions they had posed.'

After the rejection of the Constitution by Datchanina Farm and Frantsiya Farm, the burning question was, which farm would be the first to break ranks and admit the process should be stopped? Playing to two audiences, Scratcher did not cancel, but rather, immediately postponed the Belostrovo Vote of Confidence until every other farm had ratified, not daring to go against the wishes of the majority of the Combine after the humiliation brought on him by his former ally. The Chairs publicly dismissed the two Votes of Confidence as 'dangerous and stupid' and called for a 'period of reflection'. Secretly extremely relieved, Scratcher used this pause as an opportunity. He immediately announced that he was banning Votes of Confidence on Belostrovo, by order of Korolsky, for anything other than an outright proposal to dissolve the farm and transfer the title of all its land and movable assets to the Combine.

The following year, when the Frantsiya Farm animals, with some hidden encouragement from the Combine, had safely disposed of their corrupt Chair at the next Animal Committee election, Muddy moved again. The reality was that the Combine had already become so pervasive in the management of the farms and the lives of the animals, that there was no real need for a brand-new Constitution. Over the previous year, during the period of reflection and even further back than that, the Combine's control of the farms had been perfectly adequate without it. This was the real issue with the Constitution's rejection by Frantsiya and Datchanina Farms – to a great extent, it merely recorded the powers which had been already transferred to the Combine. By rejecting the Constitution, without their Chairs and the animals realising it, the two farms were actually rejecting the Combine itself.

Muddy's new plan to get them to ratify it was simple. It would no longer be a known as a 'Constitution', but instead would become the 'Fifth Annex' to the existing constitution. This was all it really ever had been - Abraham had built his foundations well, they had outlasted Krasnaya Farm, and would last many, many more years too.

On Frantsiya Farm, the day before the new Vote of Confidence, the Chair laid out the former new Constitution and the Fifth Annex side by side. As he glanced back and forth from one document to the other, he could no longer tell which was which. But it no longer mattered, the Frantsiya Farm animals had had enough of being called stupid by their betters, and narrowly agreed to it.

Almost all the Chairs came together to sign the Fifth Annex at a special ceremony. As they sat round Klemansky's old table at the Barleyfield office, they raised their glasses and toasted their cleverness in turning the Constitution into an Annex to deceive the ordinary animals. They had to constantly praise each other now, because without any vetoes, real debate had come to an end at the Council meetings. It was easier to conform to the majority view, as this was told to them by the Secretariat, than to waste time and energy trying to change a pre-ordained outcome.

Not all the Chairs were present for the ceremony and the toast. Angus had joined late, using one of the many back doors to the office, so he could avoid being seen publicly going to add his hoofprint to the document. All was not well on Belostrovo - having been promised a Vote of Confidence by the former Chair, Scratcher, on the Constitution, most of the animals felt cheated, and vowed their revenge one day. But now that the Constitution was a mere Annex, Angus claimed that the promise was void. Scratcher, for his part, cared little. He had tired of the unwillingness of any animal in the county to listen to, let alone understand Tertiary Deviationism, so had resigned as Chair, going to the neighbouring counties to be paid to explain his philosophy there.

Angus shook his forelock as he made his mark on the Annex, he did not understand why the ordinary animals were upset at being denied their Vote of Confidence and did not understand why they were so opposed to a simple Common Bartering arrangement with the neighbouring farms. And he thought it was no business of the ordinary animals to ask questions about the mountain of edicts filed in the Belostrovo farmhouse attic storeroom. This was somewhat unreasonable of him, after all, the animals had a right to know why fifteen locked cabinets of edicts had suddenly crashed through the first-floor ceiling of the farmhouse one day, into the Committee Room below. The table at which the Belostrovo Animal Committee had used to sit and deliberate was smashed to pieces, but the Committee members did not seem too perturbed, as the room was not much used these days anyway. Indeed, their main concern was simply to win re-election each year to the Committee and carry on receiving their triple Equal Rations (thanks to Standardisation this was their right, as it was the same quantity now allocated to the Combine's own Animal Committee).

Even in his short time as Chair, Angus had learned much from the Combine's Secretariat and had come to despise the lower animals (which had not been the case with him in the past). He especially despised those heretics who suggested that life without the Combine's edicts might somehow be freer, reminding them that, outside the Combine, half the animals would certainly starve to death.

But even if some of the ordinary animals were still not too scared to think such dangerous thoughts (doubly dangerous, because outside the Combine the half that did not starve would revert to Wildness), the Belostrovo Animal Committee were. They had forgotten the power of free-thinking, the art of debate and the pleasurable challenge of drawing up their own regulations to solve their own problems - these things were now almost entirely taken care of by the Combine.

The fact that the Combine had progressed to doing these things, confirmed to them rather, that the idea of all the animals from one farm, higher and lower, jointly running their own affairs and making their own decisions was an archaic, primitive practice. As something clearly contradictory to Pan-animalism, it simply could never be allowed by responsible higher animals on any farm, ever again.

As the Combine's latest motto, embroidered around

the edge of the Green Flag, said: 'THE COMBINE SAVES US FROM OURSELVES.'

Acknowledgements

Christopher Booker & Richard North, 2005 & 2016: *The Great Deception: The Secret History of the European Union*

George Orwell, 1945: *Animal Farm: A Fairy Story*

John Reed, 2015: *Revisionist History*, Harper's Magazine

Printed in Great Britain
by Amazon

28828958R00069